War

Louis-Ferdinand Céline

Translated by Sander Berg

ALMA CLASSICS

ALMA CLASSICS
an imprint of

ALMA BOOKS LTD
Thornton House
Thornton Road
Wimbledon Village
London SW19 4NG
United Kingdom
www.almaclassics.com

War first published in French as *Guerre* in 2022
© Éditions Gallimard, 2022
This translation first published by Alma Classics in 2024
Translation, notes and glossary © Sander Berg, 2024

Cover: Nathan Burton

Printed in Great Britain by CPI Group (UK) Ltd, Croydon CR0 4YY

ISBN: 978-1-84749-916-5

Contents

Other books by LOUIS-FERDINAND CÉLINE
published by Alma Classics

Death on Credit

Guignol's Band

Journey to the End of the Night

London Bridge

Introduction

Louis-Ferdinand Destouches was born in Courbevoie, in the region of Paris, in 1894 to lower-middle-class parents. They later moved to the Passage Choiseul, near the Opéra, where they ran a shop. After several apprenticeships and nine months in England to learn the language, he joined the *cuirassiers* (cavalry) shortly before the outbreak of the First World War. He was wounded in October 1914. As a result, he suffered from radial nerve paralysis in his arm, vertigo, auditory hallucinations and tinnitus, as well as what we would now call PTSD. These symptoms would stay with him for the rest of his life. He was discharged, and in May 1915 he went to London, where he spent a year in the company of French pimps and prostitutes and married a dancer.

He subsequently worked in Cameroon, studied medicine, was employed by the League of Nations, researching tuberculosis and public health, travelled in Europe and North America before settling down in the suburbs of Paris to work as a doctor treating the poor. His experiences of the war, Africa, the United States and the *banlieue* laid the foundation for his first novel, *Journey to the End of the Night* (*Voyage au bout de la nuit*, 1932), published under the pen name Louis-Ferdinand Céline, which met with huge critical acclaim. His second novel, *Death on Credit* (*Mort à crédit*, 1936), was a fantastical and picaresque reworking of his youth and marked the next step in the development of his unique style.

Had he died in 1936, Céline would have been universally hailed as one of France's very best writers of the twentieth century, up there with Proust, whose antithesis he is. However, shortly after the publication of *Death on Credit*, he destroyed his reputation for ever by writing three virulently anti-Semitic pamphlets. He spent the war in the company of French fascists and Nazi sympathizers, sending occasional letters to far-right journals, although he himself remained a contrarian non-conformist with an anarchist streak, claiming he had never voted and did not believe in man.

In 1944 he fled his home in Montmartre and embarked on a long journey through Germany as the Third Reich collapsed all around him, spending five months in Sigmaringen with members of the Vichy regime. He eventually made his way to Denmark, where he soon found himself in prison, with the French post-war government demanding his extradition. These experiences formed the basis of his German trilogy: *From Castle to Castle, North (D'un château l'autre)*and *Rigadoon (Rigodon)*. He was eventually pardoned and returned to France, where he lived as a recluse with his wife Lucette and his dogs. He died in Meudon in 1961.

* * *

The story of *War (Guerre)* is worthy of a detective novel. Written around 1934, it was not published until 2022. After the success of *Journey to the End of the Night*, the author mentioned in a letter to his publisher that he was working on a trilogy called "Childhood–War–London". For a long time it was impossible to know how much of the trilogy he had actually written, but it was clear he decided to concentrate on the first part, which led to the publication of *Death on Credit*. In 1949 he published a fragmentary novel about his time as a recruit with the cavalry, called *Cannon Fodder* (*Casse-pipe*). A few years earlier, in 1944, he had published a novel set in London during the First World War entitled *Guignol's Band*. It was tempting to assume that these works started life as the second and third part of the trilogy, even if *Cannon Fodder* is not set during the war.

Then, in 2021, *Le Monde* announced that the journalist Jean-Pierre Thibaudat had in his possession a chest containing 6,000 handwritten pages by Céline. While alive, the writer had often railed against the disappearance of many of his manuscripts, including "two or three novels", claiming they had been stolen from his flat by a certain Oscar Rosembly.

Thibaudat later confessed that he had had the documents for at least fifteen years before making public their existence. He had been given them by the daughter of Yvon Morandat, a member of the Resistance, who had occupied Céline's vacated flat sometime after he had fled. It appears that Morandat later offered Céline to take back his furniture as well as the manuscripts, provided he paid for the cost of the storage. Céline, in the account of Thibaudat, scoffed, refused to pay and said it only concerned a few rough drafts.

Thibaudat had given his word never to hand over the documents to Céline's widow, and it was not until after she had passed away at the age of 107 in 2019 that the secret came out.

In 2022 *War* was published by Gallimard. We will never know how it would have looked had Céline decided to prepare it for publication. Some of the passages no doubt would not have survived. The writing style is now reminiscent of *Journey to the End of the Night*, now of *Death on Credit*, and in places more crude than either. It is an imperfect novel, but it has a number of features that redeem it from being of mere literary-historical value. It is a powerful and also darkly comical work that contains haunting descriptions of a Flemish town in time of war, its peaceful surrounding fields, the endless stream of soldiers and *matériel*, the ubiquitous sound of field artillery, the need for sex and drink, the fear of being sent back to the front, the incapacity of those at home to comprehend the sheer horror of it all, the trauma, the suffering. It lacks the seriousness of Jünger's *Storm of Steel* and the humanity of Remarque's *All Quiet on the Western Front*, but it deserves a place in the canon of First World War novels written by those who survived it. That is, if you can accept that it was written by a man who was later to hold despicable views, and if it is possible to ever separate the writer from his work. But that is a discussion for another place and another time.

Note on the Text

The manuscript of *War* consists of numbered sequences starting with 10 and followed by 1, 2, 2', 3 and 4. These form a cohesive narrative with a clear plot, even though there are many corrections and the names of some of the characters are not fixed. The narrator's friend is initially referred to as Bébert, later as Cascade; his mother is called Célestine but also Clémence, and so on. The last chapter links to the start of *London* (*Londres*), another of the recently resurfaced novels. There seems to be a significant section missing at the start, presumably chapters 1-9. These must have contained the story of Ferdinand and his comrades, whose ghosts appear at the end of the first sequence and who also feature in *Cannon Fodder*. Their regiment is led by Le Drellière, and they are possibly attempting to desert and run off with the regiment's funds. Throughout the novel, Ferdinand fears the truth of the matter may be found out.

Note on the Translation

There is a short story by Borges called 'Pierre Menard, Author of the Quixote', in which a twentieth-century Frenchman gives himself the task to write (not translate: write) Cervantes's masterpiece. He learns seventeenth-century Spanish and imitates various aspects of the author's life before sitting down to pen the famous novel. It is a painstaking process. When he dies, he has only finished a few dozen pages, but... they are word for word the same as the original. *Mutatis mutandis*, the same can be said about translation. Having studied the source text in forensic detail, a translator could decide that the only way to do justice to all the semantic nuances, lexical ambiguities and cultural connotations of a word or expression is to keep the original. But that would be absurd. And it wouldn't be a translation. Translating is making choices: lexical, grammatical, stylistic. It is an act of re-creation, of invention. Of course you lose a lot in the process, but you can recoup some of the losses.

Translating Céline's *War* poses significant challenges. The novel has come to us in an unredacted state. There are quite a few unclear passages and many illegible words. And even if the words are clear, in some instances the exact meaning remains elusive; in a number of cases the Spanish, Italian, Dutch and German translators have come up with different interpretations of the same passage. Sometimes a seemingly innocuous word can be a real headache, because it cannot mean what it literally says, and it is not a known expression or slang. At least, not as far as one can make out. You can't ask the author. Native speakers are just as stumped, so you cross your fingers and opt for something that is plausible and fits the context.

In his novels, especially those published after *Journey to the End of the Night*, Céline made a conscious attempt to evoke the way French is spoken by the people, as opposed to the centuries-old tradition of polished written French. His style became famous for the elaborate use of ellipsis, although this is not much in evidence yet in *War*, and a preponderance of argot as well as a radically different syntax.

The most important choice a translator has to make is that of style and register. The worst thing one can do to a text by Céline would be to make it bland. It would be a betrayal of the original intent, giving truth to the Italian dictum *traduttore traditore*. And yet, it is not uncommon to see translations of Céline, including of *War*, that are written in standard grammar, even if they contain many colloquial expressions and turns of phrase. It is the safest option, offering the smoothest reading experience.

I have opted for a more radical approach, with all the risks that it entails. The tone and style of the original vary considerably. Some passages are akin to what we find in *Journey to the End of the Night*, hard-hitting but grammatically fairly standard prose, commonly used when the author steps back from the narrative and imparts his granite truths about the world. There are also some snippets of lyrical prose, beautifully evocative and original passages. But most of the novel is written in substandard French. Céline nearly always drops the "*ne*" in negatives and the "*il*" in "*il fallait*" and "*il y avait*", uses the relative pronoun "*que*" instead of "*qui*", reduplicates nouns with pronouns, uses "*que*" after question words, "*avoir*" as an auxiliary verb with reflexives, and so on. To replicate this each time it occurs with an equivalent substandard English expression is impossible. But one way to think about translation is that it is the act of imagining what someone would have said in the same situation in a different language. A sensible way of reproducing Céline's style, therefore, is to introduce comparable substandard expressions throughout in English: double negatives, "ain't", "was" instead of "were", "cos" for "because", and so on. That way, the reader of the English text will have an experience that roughly parallels that of the French reading public.

The same is true for vocabulary. Céline is writing about the First World War in the early 1930s. He uses a lot of argot. So much so that French editions have a glossary in the back of the book to explain the meaning of the slang words to French readers. My choice has been to use predominantly British slang. Essentially this is because I can only write what I would be able to produce in actual speech. And I don't speak First World War English or 1930s English. I have used some Cockney rhyming slang to give a certain flavour, especially to the character of Bébert, a Parisian pimp. Then there are expressions that are typical of the military in general and the First World War in particular. My overriding objective has been to create a particular linguistic impression; the translation does not aim for, much less claim, historical-linguistic accuracy.

Apart from the more specific uses of slang, I have attempted to convey the sheer range of insults and derogatory terms used in the text, including many words for head, face, man, woman, prostitute, copulation, penis, vagina, etc. Almost inevitably, there are also a few racial slurs. In this context it has to be remembered that slang is by its very nature subversive and transgressive, and it is not the translator's job to bowdlerize the text.

Céline's short novel is vulgar, crude, rich, funny, irreverent, shocking, harsh, lyrical, dark and powerful. And so should the translation be, warts and all.

Sander Berg
Harrow on the Hill
November 2023

War

Not quite.* I must have been lying there part of the following night too. The whole of my left ear was glued to the ground with blood, my mouth too. In between, there was a tremendous noise. I'd slept through that noise and then it had rained, a very dense rain. Next to me Kersuzon was lying heavy and stiff under water. I moved an arm towards his body. I touched him. I couldn't move my other arm. No idea where it was. It'd been flung up high into the air, whirled around up there and come down again, tugging at the raw flesh of my shoulder. It made me scream each time, which only made it worse. Later, though still crying out, I managed to make less noise than that horrendous din that was destroying my head, inside, like a train. No use rebelling against it. It was the first time I'd slept in that muck, with artillery shells whistling by on all sides, through as much noise as you can imagine, without conking out completely, that's to say, in the middle of the horror of it all. Except for the times when they operated on me, I've never completely lost consciousness again. I've always slept with that horrific noise since December 1914. I caught the war in my head. It's trapped inside my head.

Right. So I was saying that in the middle of the night I rolled over onto my belly. That wasn't too bad. I'd learnt to tell the difference between noises from the outside and noises that would stay with me for ever. As for the pain, my shoulder and my knee were hurting like hell too. All the same, I managed to get up. After all, I was actually really starving. I looked around a bit in the kind of barnyard where we'd come to a sticky end with Le Drellière and his convoy. Where would he be right now? And the others? Many hours, a whole night and almost a day had passed since we'd come to crush them. All that was left of 'em was little mounds on the hillside, while scattered across the orchard our vehicles stood smoking, crackling and smouldering. The big travelling forge was still being reduced to cinders. And the forage wagon had gone up in smoke, so to speak. I didn't recognize the adjutant in the wreckage. But I did recognize one of the horses a little further on, up against a farm wall that had just collapsed in a heap, with something dangling behind it in the ash, a bit of a shaft. They must've come back right in the middle of the shelling and broken into a gallop among the rubble, kicked up the arse and running straight into a hail of shrapnel, no two ways about it. Le Drellière really had excelled himself. I was still crouching and stayed put. The mud had been churned up proper by shellfire. At least two hundred shells had been fired at us at one point. Dead bodies left and right. The guy with the haversacks had been split open like a pomegranate, it has to be said, from his neck halfway down his trousers. Two plump rats had already made their home in his gut and were munching the stale crusts in his haversack. The barnyard smelled of burning and

4

decomposing flesh, especially the heap in the middle where a good ten horses were lying in a pile, their innards spilling out. That's where their galloping had ended, finished off by a Minnie* or three landing a couple of metres away. All of a sudden, in the complete jam I was in, my mind went back to that bag of cash Le Drellière had on him.

I still wasn't too sure what to make of it. I wasn't in a fit state to think. All the same, in spite of the horror all around, it annoyed the hell out of me, what with the deafening noise I carried around. It seemed I was the only one left at the end of our godawful adventure. The big guns in the distance, I wasn't entirely sure I actually heard them. It was all mixed up. Not too far off, I saw small groups of men on horseback and on foot moving away. I'd've liked them to be Germans, but they didn't come any closer. They had other fish to fry elsewhere, no doubt. Must've had their orders. The terrain here was probably all used up, battle-wise. So now it was up to me to find my regiment all by myself. But where could they be? Just thinking about it, even a little, I had to start over again and again, like when you're talking to someone on a platform and a train passes by. One thought at a time, concentrating very hard, one after the other. That, I can assure you, is tiring. Now I've got used to it. Twenty years will teach you. My soul has hardened, like a biceps. I no longer believe anything comes easy. I've learnt to make music, sleep, forgive and, as you can see, create beautiful literature too, with little bits of horror wrested from that never-ending noise. But enough of that.

In the wreckage of the big travelling forge there was tins of bully beef. They'd exploded in the fire, but were good enough for me. Except I got thirsty. What I ate with my one hand was covered in blood, mine, naturally, and others' too. Anyhow, I started to look for a corpse that might have some booze on it. I found one, a light cavalryman at the far end, near the entry to the barnyard. He had some wine in his coat, two whole bottles of the stuff. Nicked, no doubt. Officers' claret. After that, I headed east, back to where we came from. For about a hundred metres. I could clearly sense I was starting to see things. I thought I saw a horse in the middle of a field. I wanted to get on it, but when I got close, it turned out to be nothing more than a bloated cow which had been dead for three days. This made me even more tired, of course. Soon I began seeing pieces of artillery that couldn't have been there. Things were no longer the same, what with my ear and all.

I still hadn't come across any actual *poilus*. A few more kilometres. I swallowed more blood. Noise-wise it was calming down a bit in my head. But then I threw everything up, including the two bottles of wine. Everything was spinning. For fuck's sake, Ferdinand, I told myself. You ain't going to cop it now you've done the hardest bit, are you?

I've never been so brave. And then I thought of the money bag, of all the regiment's looted vans, and it hurt three times over, my arm, my whole horrible noise-filled head and, deeper still, my conscience. I panicked, cos deep down I'm a good lad. I'd have spoken out loud to myself if the blood hadn't made my tongue stick. That usually gives me strength.

It's flat country over there – but those treacherous ditches, deep and filled with water, made the going very tough. I had to make endless detours only to end up on the same spot.

I kept thinking I heard bullets whistling by. Still, the cattle trough where I stopped must've been real. I held my bad arm with the other, cos I could no longer keep it straight. It was hanging dead by my side. At the height of the shoulder, it was one big spongy mass of fabric and blood. If I moved it just a little, it all but killed me, the atrocious pain getting to within an inch of my life, no two ways about it.

I felt there was still plenty of life inside, though, hanging in there, as 't were. If someone had told me, I'd have never thought it possible. I was even making steady progress on foot now. Well, two hundred metres at a time. I was in excruciating pain all over, from below the knee to the inside of my head. Plus my ear was one big mush of sounds. Things weren't the same or anything like before. Everything seemed made of putty – wobbly trees, the road moving up and down beneath my boots. I was covered only by my tunic and the rain. Still no one. The torture in my head was getting louder in the wide and open fields. I nearly got scared listening to myself. I kept thinking it might kick off another battle, that's how much noise there was inside. In my head there was more noise than a battle. In the distance, lit up by a sunbeam, I saw an actual bell tower rising up beyond the fields – it was massive. Go there, I told myself. It's as good a destination as any. And then I sat down, with that infernal racket in my bonce and my arm in tatters, and I tried to remember what had just happened. I couldn't. It was one big blur, memory-wise. And on top of that, I was too hot, and even the bell tower kept changing its distance, piercing my eyes now up close, now far away. Maybe it's a mirage, I told myself. But I'm not that stupid. Since I hurt like hell all over, the bell tower must exist as well. It's a way of reasoning, of having something to believe in. I was off again, walking on the side of the road. On one of my detours I spotted a guy moving about in the muck below. I was sure he'd seen me. A wriggling corpse, I thought to myself. Surely I was imagining things. He was dressed in yellow and carried a rifle. I'd never seen anyone in that kind of gear. The guy was shaking, or perhaps it was me. He signalled me to come nearer. So I got nearer. I had nothing to lose. Then he spoke to me up close like. I recognized his language immediately. It was an Englishman. Given my state, I thought he might be a figment of my imagination. But without even having to think about it and despite the blood in my mouth, I quickly replied in English. There's me, who hadn't wanted to utter even a handful of words when I was there to learn the language, striking up a conversation with this guy in yellow. Must've been the emotion, no doubt. It even did my ear good to talk to him in English. The noise seemed to calm down. Then he helped me to walk. He supported me with great care. I had to pause every other step. Better to be found by him than by one of our own stupid bastards, I thought. At least I didn't have to tell him the whole shebang, about the war and how our expedition had ended.

"*Where are we going?*"* I asked him…

"To Yprèss!"* he replied.

Yprèss, that must be that bell tower over there. So it was an actual bell tower of an actual town. Hopping along as I was, it would still be another four hours on foot, along paths and, above all, through fields. I couldn't see very clearly. Plus, I saw everything through a red haze. I'd divided my body up in various parts. The drenched part, the drunk part, the part of the arm, which was atrocious, the part of the ear, which was unbearable, the part of the friendship I felt for the Englishman, which was consoling, the part of the knee, which went off in all directions, the part of the past, which I clearly remember was trying to connect to the present and failing – and then there was the part of the future, which scared me more than the rest put together, and at last a funny old part that wanted above all to tell me a story. You couldn't even call it misery, it was just funny. We walked for another kilometre or so and then I refused to carry on.

"Where was you headed?" I asked him all of a sudden, out of curiosity I guess.

I stopped. I refused to budge. Even though that Ypres of his wasn't far off. The fields around us were rolling. Big, heaving bumps swelling up as if giant rats were pushing up clods of earth as they moved about underground. Could even have been people. It was huge, like an army skimming along the surface of the earth... Rolling like the sea, like actual waves.... I'd better sit down and stay put... Especially with those thunderstorms raging between my ears. The inside of my head was one big hurricane. Suddenly I let out an enormous roar.

"*I am not going! I am going to the* War of Movement!"*

And that's exactly what I did. I got up, what with my arm and ear and blood everywhere, and set off in the direction of the enemy, back to where we came from. My companion had a right go at me, and I got every word he said. My fever must've gone up. The hotter I was, the easier I found it to understand English. I was limping, but pig-headedly continued with my act of bravery. He couldn't figure out how to stop me. So we kind of had a row in the middle of the plain. Thankfully there was no one there to see us. In the end he won. He grabbed me by the arm, the one in tatters. That way he was bound to get the better of me. I followed him. But we hadn't walked for more than a quarter of an hour in the direction of the town when I saw about ten horsemen in khaki coming down the road towards us. Seeing them up close I began to imagine things, that the fighting was about to kick off again.

"*Hurray!*" I bellowed as soon as I saw them in the distance. "*Hurray!*"

I could tell they were English.

"*Hurray!*" came their reply.

Their officer approached. He paid me a compliment.

"*Brave soldier! Brave soldier!*" he said. "*Where do you come from?*"*

I hadn't really thought about where I was coming from.* That bastard made me relive all my fears.

I wanted to skedaddle in two directions at once, ahead and back. My companion, who'd taken charge of me, suddenly gave me a great kick up the backside in the direction of the town. No one wanted me to be brave. I couldn't figure out where I wanted to go, forwards or backwards, and on the inside it was hurting like hell. Le Drellière hadn't seen any of this. He died too soon. At one point the road actually rose up towards me, very gently, like a kiss, as 't were, right up to the height of my eyes, and I laid myself down on it like on a soft bed with that massive barrage continuing inside my skull and everything. Then it all calmed down, and the horses of the men in khaki came back towards me, or at least I heard their stupid galloping, as I didn't see a soul.

When I came to, I was in a church, on a real bed. Once again the noise in my ears had woken me up, as well as that of a dog I thought was eating my left arm. I just gave up. Apart from someone rooting around in my guts without anaesthetic, I couldn't be in more pain. The ordeal didn't just last one hour, it lasted the whole night. In the darkness my eyes caught a glimpse of a strange movement, soft and melodious, that seemed to stir something inside of me.

I couldn't believe it. It was the arm of some bint. Despite my state, it tickled something in my dick. With one eye I checked out her buttocks. I saw how she wiggled her arse, this way and that, between the bedsteads, stretching the fabric of her skirt. It was like a dream starting all over again. Life's full of stuff like that. All sorts of ideas tumbled into my head, all muddled up. Like good lads, they followed that backside expectantly. They moved me to a corner of the church where there was lots of light. There I conked out again, because of something they made me smell, I imagine. They wanted to put me to sleep. Two days must've passed, with tremendous noises and more pain in my swollen head than actual life. It's funny I should remember those days. What's stuck in my memory is not the pain I felt, but no longer being responsible for anything, not even my own carcass, like some helpless idiot. It was beyond unbearable, it was embarrassing. This whole person you get given and stick up for, your uncertain, grisly past, already hardened, your body falling to pieces and running after its bits – it all becomes ridiculous in those moments. I was watching life getting ready to torment me. But when I'm in the throes of death, I'll spit it right in the face. From a certain point onwards, life becomes a load of bollocks. No use having me on. I know about life. I've got my eye on it. We'll have it out one day. We've got a bone to pick. Fuck life!

But I'd better tell the whole story. After three days, a shell exploded on the main altar, a real one. The English in charge of the field hospital decided we all had to go. I wasn't particularly fussed. The church was full of movement too. Pillars twisting like marshmallow cables at a fair in the yellow and green light of the stained-glass windows. We drank lemonade from baby bottles. In a way, it was all fine and dandy. I mean as far as liquids passing through was concerned. I had a nightmare in which I even saw General Métuleu des Entrayes up there in the vaults, riding a winged horse of solid gold. No doubt looking for me… He spotted me and tried to remember who I was. Then his mouth moved and his moustache started to flutter like a butterfly.

"I've changed, haven't I, Métuleu?" I asked him quietly, as if we were mates.

And then, in spite of everything, I fell asleep, but with an added unease, very pronounced, right in between my eye sockets, lodged deep in my thoughts, beyond even that noise I keep on banging on about, tremendous though it was.

They transported us safely to the station and put us all on a train. It was cattle wagons, still reeking of fresh manure. The train chugged along slowly. Not so long ago we'd come from the opposite direction, to fight. That was one, two, three, four months ago already. There was just two rows of stretchers along the length of the wagon. I was close to the doors. There was another smell too, the smell of corpses, I knew it well, and of phenol. They'd had to evacuate the field hospital in a great hurry.

"Moo... Moo!" I lowed like a cow as soon as I woke up, cos it was the place for it.

At first no one answered. We crept ahead, step by step, as 't were. After three times, two guys at the back replied:

"Moo! Moo!" That's a good cry for the wounded. Trips off the tongue easy like.

Choo! Choo!... in the distance. Must be the engine going up a slope. The explosions in my ear no longer fooled me. We stopped next to a river that flowed from the moon. Then, with a judder, we were on our way again. In short, it was almost the same as it had been coming from the other direction. It reminded me of Péronne. I was wondering what other pongos might be lying here, in these cattle wagons, and if they were French, English or Belgian perhaps.

"Moo, moo!" is a language people from all over understand, so I tried again.

No reply this time. The moaners were just moaning more loudly. Except one guy who kept on repeating "Marie" with a strong accent, and then, very close to me, something that sounded like *gloo gloo*. Some geezer choking on his own blood, no doubt. I recognized the sound. In two months, I'd learnt almost all the sounds of earth and men. Then we stood still on an embankment for a good two hours, in the freezing cold. Just the *choo choo* of the engine. And then a cow in a field ahead of us started to low, *moo moo*, a lot louder than I had. I answered to see what'd happen. It must have been hungry. We moved a little, *brroom, brroom...* All the wheels, all the flesh, all the ideas of the world, it was all jumbled up with the noise deep inside my head. It was then I told myself it was over. That's it. I put my foot on the floor. It held. I swivelled round. Even managed to sit up. I peered into the darkness of the wagon, in front, behind. My eyes got used to the dark. I saw bodies that weren't moving, covered by blankets, lying on stretchers. Two rows of 'em.

"Moo, moo," I said.

No one responded. I was able to stand up. Not for long, but long enough to make it to the doors. With one arm I opened them a little further... I sat down in the opening, in the darkness of the night. It was exactly like when we'd come to the front, except that now we were going even more slowly. Plus there was no horses in the wagons. It must've been very cold. It was long past summer, but I was hot and thirsty as if it had been summer, and I was seeing things in the dark. On account of my noises, I even heard voices and then whole columns marching through the fields, less than two metres above the soil. It was their turn all right. They were all on their way to the front. I was on my way back. Our wagon was on the small side, but I reckon there was at least fifteen corpses. Maybe you could still hear field guns in the distance. It was probably the same in the other wagons. *Choot! Choot!* It was only a little engine, and it was struggling to pull the whole caboodle. We were going backwards. If I stay with these bods, I told myself, I'll die for sure, but I was in so much pain and there was so much noise in my head that in a sense it might be a relief. Then suddenly I could make out the face of the corpse on a stretcher at the back, on the right, and the faces of the others too. The wagon had stopped right underneath a gas lamp-post. I felt like saying something to them.

"Moo, moo!" I told all of them.

Then the train was crawling through the countryside again. The fields were covered by a fog so dense, I told myself: Ferdinand, you're going to walk across as if you was at home.

So I did. I stepped straight onto the eiderdown, so to speak. I wrapped myself in clouds. This is it, I told myself, this time I'll desert for good. I sat down. It was wet. A bit further I could already see the walls of a town, high city walls, with a real, strong castle protecting it. A great northern town, no doubt. I told myself, I'll sit down in front of it. Now that I was safe, I was no longer alone. A mischievous look came over me. There was Kersuzon, Keramplech, Gargader and the kid Le Cam,* all around me, forming a circle, as 't were. Except that they had their eyes shut. They were reproaching me. In a word, they'd come to watch over me. After almost four years together! And yet I never told them any tales. Gargader was bleeding profusely from the middle of his forehead. It tainted the fog below him all red. I even told him so. Kersuzon, it's true, had no arms, but he had big ears the better to hear me with. As for the kid Le Cam, you could see straight through his skull, through his eyes, like a pair of binoculars. It was a scream. Keramplech had grown himself a beard. He had long hair like a lady. He'd kept his helmet on and was cleaning his nails with the point of his bayonet. He was there to hear me out too. His guts were spilling out of his arse, all over the countryside. I had to speak to them, if not they'd rat me out for sure. The fighting's in the north, I told them. That's where it's at, it ain't here at all. But they kept shtoom.

King Krogold went back home.* Just as I was saying that, the sound of field artillery boomed across the fields. I pretended not to hear it. It ain't real, I said. The four of us sang together. King Krogold has come home! We were singing out of tune. I spat on Kersuzon's face, which was completely red. That's when the idea came to me. It was beautiful. We were standing outside of Christianie. That's my opinion, even now. On the road, somewhere down south that is, Thibaut and Joad were making their way towards me. They were wearing weird old uniforms, mere rags, to be honest. They were also coming from Christianie, looking for loot, perhaps. You'll all come down with a fever, you scumbags, I shouted. Kersuzon and the others didn't dare contradict me. After all, I was a corporal, even after everything that had happened. Desertion or not, it was up to me to know the truth. I had to know everything.

"Tell me," I said to Gargader Yvon, who was from around there. "It was Thibaut who killed Morvan, Joad's old man. Just say it. It was him what killed him. Tell me," I said to him. "Tell me everything, right from the start, I mean. Tell me how he killed him. With a dagger? A piece of rope? A sabre? No? With a big stone, then? Bashing his face in."

"That's true," Gargader replied. "That's exactly it, word for word."

Old Morvan had lent him some money to shut him up and not take away his son on some faraway adventure, to leave him be and let him spend his life by his side in Terdigonde, in the Vendée, just like us, when we got bored stiff with the

22nd in Romanches on the Somme, way back, before the war. One day, Joad's old man must've invited a bunch of powerful and very well-off people, local magistrates, who got shitfaced at his house. Old Morvan was sozzled too, even a bit more than the rest, so much so he had to puke. He left his seat at the dinner table to lean out of the window. In the alleyway below, there was no one yet. What there was, was a little cat and a big stone. Thibaut was arriving just around the corner.

"Your friend ain't coming. Your friend won't come and entertain us, play his instrument for us, even though I paid him. He asked for an advance of twenty *écus*... He's a thief, is Thibaut, I've always said it."

That's when Thibaut, who'd overheard him, got up with the big stone in his hand and killed old Morvan dead with a single blow to the temple. An insult well and truly avenged. Terrible. Just like that his soul left him, flying heavenward like the knell of a heavy bell on the first stroke.

Thibaut and his men entered the house. Three days later, they buried the public prosecutor. Old mother Morvan was distraught and never suspected a thing. Thibaut moved into the dead man's room, as if he was a friend. Him and Joad visited all the pubs for miles around. Until one day the two of them had their fill. Joad could only think of faraway lovers, of Princess Wanda, King Krogold's daughter out on the heights of Morehande, even further north than Christianie. Thibaut only wanted adventures. Even the wealthy household couldn't keep him back. He'd killed in vain, for the hell of it. And so the two of them left. We see them crossing Brittany, like Gargader before them.

17

They're leaving Terdigonde in the Vendée for good, just like Keramplech.

"Isn't that a lovely story I just told you?..." I asked my three disgusting bods.

Initially they didn't say a word, but in the end it was Cambelech who snuck up behind me when I wasn't expecting it. His mouth was wide open, split into two, with the lower jaw dangling down over his revolting rags.

"Corporal," he said, using both his hands to move his mouth... "We ain't happy. The last thing we need is stories like that..."*

I was completely and utterly knocked out. But life clung on doggedly, cos it wasn't until two days later that they picked me up, lying in a meadow, at the foot of the embankment where I'd let myself slip off the train. I was still raving, that's for sure. They took me to a hospital. They had to make up their minds before making a decision. They couldn't work out if I was Belgian or English, and weren't convinced I was French neither. I was wearing so many different bits of kit, all picked up along the way. I could've been German and they'd've been none the wiser. And there was hospitals to suit all tastes in Peurdu-sur-la-Lys. It was a small town, but ideally located to receive squaddies from just about every battlefield. They stuck a bunch of labels on my belly, and I ended up being sent to the Virginal Secours on the Rue des Trois-Capucines, which was run by society ladies as well as nuns. Hardly the most reputable of destinations, as will become clear. In a sense it pissed me off I was doing better, cos I had to make an effort to keep bullshitting them as they transported me. It was no longer as sincere. In the end, those two days and two nights in the grass had done me a world of good. Some fucking vitality. I squinted from my stretcher to look at the geezers carrying me into town. White-haired orderlies they were. As for the pain, the noise, the whistling, the whole infernal racket, it had all come straight back as soon as I regained consciousness, but it was bearable. In short, I preferred being that wreck I was before, when I was as good as dead, just a shitty heap of pain, music and ideas. Now it was clear that if they asked me a question, I just had to reply. That could get serious, never mind all the blood in my mouth and that big wadge of cotton wool blocking my left ear. That dream stuff about the legend, I no longer had the cheek to palm it off and serve it up to them, cos now I had the shivers. I was as cold as a corpse, but just that: cold. Things weren't going well. They gingerly carried me across a proper drawbridge and through the gates of the town. We passed officers and even a general, then Englishmen, lots of guys in khaki, and bistros, hairdressers. And horses being led to a cattle trough, which brought back a thousand memories. Looking at all of this reminded me of Romanches. How many months since we left? It felt like the world had changed around us, as if we'd fallen off the moon...

Still, I took it all in, this new place. I couldn't have ended up more ugly and repulsive, and yet I was wary as hell. After all, those arseholes still had it in for this ignorant piece of shit, this bleeding lump of meat, this howling ear, this capitulating fathead, and I was sure they'd hunt me down and there'd be no escape.

"Well, Ferdinand," I told myself, "you should've died before now, you're a right coward, a fucking wastrel, too bad for you, you bell end."

I wasn't far off. I have a gift for imagination, I can say that without pissing anyone off. Neither am I afraid of reality, but what was going on in Peurdu-sur-la-Lys would be [...]* enough to lower the fever of entire battalions. Don't ask. I'll explain. You be the judge. In these cases, too, you give yourself advice. You head for what's left of your hopes. But hope hardly shines bright, just a tiny flickering candle at the far end of an endless and perfectly hostile corridor. But you make do.

"Come on in, please."

We'd arrived. The orderlies deposited me in the basement of a building.

"He's in a coma!" a quite attractive bint told them. "Leave him over there, we'll see…"

I produced some noise through my nose when I heard her say that. I got shit-scared they'd just dump me in one of those crates. I could see crates and trestle tables. Suddenly the bint reappeared.

"He's in a coma, I'm telling you!"

Then she enquired: "I hope there's nothing wrong with his bladder at least?"

That seemed like a bizarre question, doolally though I was. The fellers who'd brought me in didn't have the foggiest about my bladder. But just then I really needed a piss. I let it go, and it flowed over the stretcher and onto the glazed tiles on the floor. The bint couldn't help but notice. With a quick movement she unbuttoned my trousers. She felt my johnson. The geezers left to go and fetch some other raving bod. The bint then homed in on my trousers. Believe it or not, but I got a little hard. I didn't want to appear so dead

21

they'd shove me in a crate, but neither did I want to have such a massive hard-on that they'd take me for an impostor. Not at all. The bint fondled me so thoroughly and good that I squirmed. I took a peek. The room had white curtains with tiles on the floor. To the left and right I saw stretchers covered with stiff sheets. I was right. Just what I thought they was. Then more coffins arrived on the trestle tables. It was not the time to get things wrong.

"Make an effort, Ferdinand. You're in a real fix. You're a cheat, so cheat."

That floozie must've taken a shine to me right off the bat. She wasn't put off. She wouldn't let go of my schlong. I asked myself, should I smile or what? Do I play nice or pretend to be unconscious? In the end, I just mumbled something. That was less risky. I continued with my little song:

"I want to go to Morehande!…" I hummed through the blood clots in my mouth. "I shall go and see King Krogold… I shall go on a great crusade all by myself…"

Suddenly the bint redoubled her efforts and started to wank me off good, reassured no doubt by my nonsense, except that I hurt my arm and I writhed like a toad. I let out a little cry and then I came all over her hands. She noticed I kept my eyes shut and wiped me clean with some cotton wool. I was delirious, that was all. Some other women entered. I took a butcher's. They looked like virgins. I heard my bint say:

"You need to put a catheter in this one. Come here, miss Cotydon, you need to learn. This wounded soldier here, he's got something wrong with his bladder too… Before he left, Doctor Méconille made it very clear to us…

'Catheterize the wounded who barely urinate... Catheterize the wounded'..."

So they took me to the first floor, supposedly to insert a catheter. I was somewhat reassured. I had another squint. No coffins on the first floor. Just beds with screens around them.

Four of the women began to undress me. First they poured water over me, from top to toe, all over my rags. Everything was stuck together, from my hair to my socks. My feet were one with the leather of my boots. It really hurt to take 'em off. My arm was covered in maggots. I could see them wriggle. Feel 'em, too. Suddenly the Cotydon girl felt sick. My handjob fairy took her place. She wasn't half bad, my handjob fairy, except for her buck teeth, which were greenish with one spot that was quite rotten, but who cares. It seemed the atmosphere couldn't get any more agreeable and attentive than this. I opened both my eyes, fixing my gaze on the ceiling.

"Death to Gwendor the criminal, death to the criminal Germans... Death to the invaders of poor Belgium."

I spouted nonsense at full blast. I was being prudent. They were staring at me... There was still four of them.

"He's still delirious, the poor man. Bring me the kit. I'll insert the catheter myself," mused my handjob fairy.

"All right, miss. I'll bring the catheters to you right away."

They left me alone with that woman who got straight down to it. But seriously, she slowly scraped the inside of my schlong. It wasn't funny any more. My dick went limp. I didn't dare scream, though. Afterwards, she bandaged me. She put a new dress on my head, ear and arm, made me drink something from a spoon and then they left me alone.

"Get a rest, now," said the catheterizer-in-chief. "In a little while, Captain Boisy Jousse, our orderly officer, will come and ask you some questions, if you are in a fit state to answer them, that is. And then tonight, Doctor Méconille will come and see you…"

I had a future. I'd be nowhere near "in a fit state", as she put it. I didn't tell Boisy Jousse a thing at first. It was quite simple. For the first ten days or so they could think what they liked. I had no papers on me. All I had was my crooked, bloody mug, and the rest of me not much better and a good deal worse on the inside. That was all. I no longer dreaded getting another catheter. She was obsessed by it. Miss L'Espinasse her name was. She was in charge of the place. In the evenings, I'd have a fever. That felt good. I didn't get gangrene, although I wasn't far off. I just ponged. It was still a question whether to put me in isolation with the dying below or not. L'Espinasse was probably getting bored with my catheters and wanking me. Except one evening when the doctor didn't come. He was busy. She walked in between the beds and kissed me on the forehead, on the sly, behind the screen. I repaid her by bursting into a bit of muttered poetry… as if I was dying…

"Wanda, wait no more for your betrothed; Gwendor, for your saviour wait no more… Joad, your heart lacks courage… Thibaut, I see him coming north… Far north of Morehande. Krogold is coming… coming to take me away…"

Then I went *gloo gloo*. I even managed to spit up some blood, vigorously sucking the inside of my nose. She dabbed my nostrils with a compress and kissed me again. Deep down she was a passionate girl. I didn't really understand what made her tick, but I had a sneaking suspicion I might badly need her later on, that old bint. How right I was.

The next day, when he'd checked up on me, Doctor Méconille got all excited. He was to operate on me double quick. That very same evening, he said. L'Espinasse objected on account of my exhaustion. I think that's what saved me. If I understood it correctly, he wanted to remove the bullet from inside my ear right away. She wasn't having any of it. Just one look at Méconille convinced me that if he ever got hold of my head, I'd be a goner. As soon as he'd left, the girls around L'Espinasse told her she'd been right to resist on my behalf. "He's a doctor, not a surgeon, and he wants to operate to get the hang of it, but he's got to start with the easy cases. The war is far from over… he's got plenty of time. He'd do better, for example, to try and patch up his arm, which is broken as well, but his head, that's too difficult for him… to start off with, anyways." As for me, having been shown the little morgue in the basement on my arrival added to my terror. It had scared the bejesus out of me. Had they not shown me the tiny morgue with its trestle tables and the two coffins on it, I probably wouldn't have put up such a fight, I might have been swayed, but it was knowing this, having seen them pine overcoats, that made me fight tooth and nail. I found the morgue revolting, with its smell of rotting corpses. And I was sure that if Méconille didn't finish me off with his operation, he'd make the dizziness, hurricanes and whistling trains in my head get worse once he started to root around the mystery inside. I used it to mess around and make my suffering bearable. And I had no confidence he could make things better for me. One look at him was enough. For starters, he never took off his glasses, and wore a pince-nez to boot. His beard was bigger than his face, his tunic a couple of sizes too small so he couldn't spread his arms, his hands had hair up to his fingernails, and his puttees were sagging around his ankles. Méconille was everything that's filthy and embarrassing. No decision was taken. The next morning when he was doing the rounds he gave me a dirty look. I remained on tenterhooks. Then one morning L'Espinasse asked me very gently for my service number after all. I gave her some random number. It was none of her business. The longer it took for them to identify me, the better, I told myself. Very early the next morning I went under the ether. Although I'd had my fair share of horrible sensations, L'Espinasse treated me to yet another. She pressed the inhaler on my conk with both hands. She was a strong lass.

To begin with, I had a whale of a time, I swear. After all, they'd done so much to me already that I threw myself on the delirium inhaler with a kind of joy. As for the ringing, the ether unleashed a true private typhoon, which surprised even me. Since I'd never hear the like of it again, I plunged into that orchestral fury, like being in the heart of a locomotive. Except I felt that it was my very own heart that was the source of all that violence. So then I felt sorry for it. You've got a good heart, you have, Ferdinand, I told myself... Mustn't mistreat it... It's not nice, it's cowardly what you do... You're taking advantage...

Suddenly I wanted to rise to the surface of the noise and bash L'Espinasse's face in... But she was pushing the inhaler on my mouth, holding me down, as they say. That cow...

A way out? Fat chance!… In her tight embrace, my whole carcass turned into the clapper of a bell… Hitting her with my head… *Boom!* Smack in the eye. *Bang!* Against her ear. I nearly reached the surface… Red… On… White… She'd won, the bitch.

Right. Now let me tell you how I woke up… I heard myself scream, would you believe it?…

"Sweet boy! My sweet boy!…" louder and louder still.

That's what I'd found in infinity. I came out of this shitty nothingness with a pretty boy! I didn't even have one. Never had a pretty boy in my whole fucking life, and that's the truth. It was a nugget of tenderness I dragged back up with me, and that disgusted me hearing it up close. Then my eye caught some flowers and a screen, and I puked a great mass of bile onto my pillow. I began to writhe and pull my arm off. There was at least four of them, all men, restraining me. I threw up again. The first person I actually recognized was my mother, then my father and then, a bit further away, Miss L'Espinasse. It was all vague and blurry like the bottom of an aquarium, and then eventually everything became clear at last, and I heard my mother telling me:

"Now, now, Ferdinand. Calm down, dear…"

She cried a bit, but I could see she was embarrassed at finding me in such an unseemly state. I might have been delirious, but no one was fooling me. My father was there too, at a little distance. He'd put on his white tie and best suit for the visit.

"They've done a great job on your arm, Ferdinand," said Miss L'Espinasse. "Doctor Méconille is very happy about how the operation went."

"Oh, we're ever so grateful, miss," my mother said, barely letting her finish her sentence. "I can assure you that my son will be most thankful to him and to you too, miss, for looking after him with such devotion."

What's more, they'd brought presents from Paris, from their shop. More sacrifices. We had to show how grateful we were immediately. Sitting at the foot of my bed, my mother was still horribly embarrassed by my vomiting, my foul language, my filth, while my father thought I was once again a disgrace.

They must've found some military papers in my pockets after all, seeing as they'd been informed. The thought hit me like an icicle in the middle of my brain.

It was no joke. They stayed for a good two or three hours watching me come to. But I was in no hurry whatever to listen to them or try and understand the situation. Then my mother started to talk to me again. As my mother, she had every right to. I didn't respond. She disgusted me no end. Bloody hell, I felt like walloping her. And for a thousand and one reasons, not all of them very clear, but all fuelled by hate. Besides, I was fed up to the back teeth with reasons. My father didn't say very much. He looked mistrustful and rolled his eyes. We were at war, the war he'd always gone on about. They'd come all the way from Paris just to see me. They must've got a permit from the chief constable at Saint-Gaille. They immediately started to talk about the shop, the terrible worries they had, the business that wasn't going at all well. I couldn't hear them clearly, what with the racket in my ear, but I heard enough. It did very little to make me feel sorry for them. I gave them another good look. They were a sorry couple, those two at the foot of my bed, and clueless to boot.

"To hell with you," I finally said. "I've got nothing to say to you. Just bugger off…"

"Oh, Ferdinand!" my mother replied. "You really do hurt our feelings. You should be happy, you know. You are out of the war. You were only wounded, and with your health you will be better soon, I'm sure. The war will be over, and you'll find yourself a good position. From now on, you will be sensible, and I'm sure you'll live to a ripe old age. You have a strong constitution. Your parents are in good health. You know we have never been extravagant… You were always well looked after at home… These ladies here are good to you… We met your doctor on our way up… He speaks very kindly of you…"

I kept my mouth shut. I'd never seen or heard anything as revolting as my father and my mother. I pretended I was drifting off. They upped and left for the train station, snivelling.

"He's delirious, you know. He's just delirious," said L'Espinasse, to excuse my behaviour as she accompanied them out.

I could hear her in the corridor.

It wouldn't be long now. Misfortunes never come singly. Less than one hour later they told me Mrs Onime, our old canteen lady, was there to see me. In person. She stood at the foot of my bed too, muttering. I pretended to be delirious. She wore a little hat with a bird on it and a veil, a boa and a fur coat. Fancy stuff. She dabbed at her tears with a hanky. But I looked her straight in the eye. I knew who

I was dealing with. She was the one asking the questions, but she was pussyfooting around. First I wondered how she'd ever understand what had happened. I'd stopped thinking about it, but she made me think about it again. There was no way of explaining what happened to our expedition and how it had ended.* Things like that you've just got to sense. And that stupid cow Onime couldn't possible sense it.

"He's dead," I just said. "He died like a hero! That's all there is to it."

Her knees gave way.

"Oh, Ferdinand!" she said. "Oh, Ferdinand!"

She got up, pretended to sway and collapsed onto her knees again. She cried and buried her face in my blanket. I get very mistrustful about those sorts of things. And right I was, too. She was still crying. Miss L'Espinasse wasn't far off, somewhere behind the screen, eavesdropping no doubt. Then she appeared, her mouth pinched.

"The patients are not to be tired out, Madame. The doctor has forbidden it. The visit is over…"

Suddenly Mrs Onime got up, very annoyed and very icy.

"Ferdinand," she said out loud, so that everyone would hear her. "You haven't forgotten that when you left your quarters you had an unpaid bill of three hundred and twenty-two francs… When do you think of settling it?"

"I don't know, Madame… I don't get any pay here…"

"You don't get any pay… Well, I'll have to write to your parents again, won't I? Even though I seem to remember you gave me your word of honour you would not run up any more debts in the canteen…"

She said it to make me look bad in the eyes of L'Espinasse.
She added:

"I think I bumped into your parents on my way here.
I might still find them at the station."

And off she was like a fucking flash, flying down the
stairs... I counted to one hundred, two hundred. Within
a quarter of an hour my father was back... out of breath
and in a right state.

"Ferdinand! How come you didn't tell us? Another blow
for us. The lady who runs the canteen came up to us, right
there on the platform at the station, and demanded we pay
her a debt. A debt you owe her since you left her camp. We,
who have known nothing but deprivation and bent ourselves
over backwards to make sure you had everything you needed.
You know better than anyone what it has cost us! You've
brought us nothing but shame. But three hundred francs...
the way things stand at the moment, we are going to have to
borrow that sum and, I don't know, make yet another huge
sacrifice. Perhaps your mother will have to pawn her earrings
again. But I have undertaken to settle the debt within eight
days. I'm a man of honour, I am! Think about it, Ferdinand!
We are at war. Did that ever cross your mind? Our business
is completely ruined, and you know full well the trouble we
have... I am not even sure I'll keep my job at La Coccinelle."

He had tears in his eyes... But L'Espinasse intervened once
again. She asked him to go easy on me. He left, muttering
excuses. They probably saw each other again at the station.
Night fell.

It must have been eleven o'clock that same evening that
L'Espinasse came up expressly in order to inform me that

I'd be transferred to a communal ward with other patients the next day, cos new wounded soldiers kept on coming in. Yesterday I was doing so much better and so on and so forth, though she still reckoned I needed a catheter. It wasn't the moment for gripes or to put up a fight. I knew her game. She took the biggest catheter of the lot. It scraped like hell. It was just her inserting it. If I refuse, my instinct told me, my goose'll be well cooked. I suspected she had something else in store for me too. The whole thing lasted a good ten minutes. I cried hot tears, but not out of sentimentality.

Right. The next morning they moved me to the Saint-Gonzef ward. My bed was between Bébert and Oscar the Zouave. I won't talk about him, cos in the three weeks he was lying next to me all he did was relieve himself through a catheter. He talked about nothing else. And about his dysentery, which had him entirely in its grips, plus a gut wound he had. His belly was like vat for making jam. When it fermented too much, his catheter overflowed, and the liquid oozed onto the floor under bed. That feels good, he'd say. He would smile at everyone. A little smile. That feels so good, he'd say again. He was full of it. In the end he died with a smile on his kisser.

But Bébert to my right, well, he was something else. He hailed from Paris, like me. Except he was from the 70th bastion, near Porte Brancion.* He immediately opened new vistas to me. When I told him about my life, he reckoned it'd been hard.

"I've made my choice," he said. "I'm only nineteen and a half, but I'm married. I've made my choice."

I didn't understand straight away, but he amazed me. I thought I was good at fending for myself, but he was the dog's bollocks. At the moment he had a wound in his foot, his left toe to be exact. A nice old bullet. He was wise to L'Espinasse's games, and worse.

"I could tell you stuff about that *palone* you couldn't even begin to imagine."

He made me feel curious again, this Bébert. That was a good sign. My arm was bearable after Méconille had operated on it. I jerked off with my left hand. I was learning all the time.

But as soon as I got up, I wobbled on my feet like a bowling pin. I had to sit down every twenty steps. As for the ringing in my ears, it was like a funfair, you wouldn't believe it. It was so loud I asked Bébert if he didn't hear anything. I learnt to listen to his stories through my own racket, but he had to speak up, louder and louder. In the end we had a right larf.

"Are you eighty, or what?" he said. "You's as mutton as my Angèle's uncle. She's my treacle, she is. Her old man used to be in the navy."

Angèle was his family, his wife, legit and all. She was all he ever talked about. She was eighteen years old.

The other guys on the ward came in all shapes and sizes, with wounds on all surfaces and of all depths. Many of them reservists. Stupid bastards on the whole. Most of them left almost as soon as they entered, to earth or to heaven. At least one in three was groaning. There was maybe twenty-five of us on the Saint-Gonzef ward. But at night, at around ten, I was seeing at least one hundred wounded, so I turned over in my bed and tried to keep my trap shut so as not to wake the others. I was shaking with tremendous deliriums. The next morning I asked Bébert if he'd ever seen L'Espinasse come to my bed on purpose to give me a good old wank as soon as I started to rave. No, he said. He was being cautious. But I knew I wasn't completely imagining it. Time passed. In the end I was on the best of terms with L'Espinasse. I was doing well. Her green teeth never really frightened me. And she did have magnificent, plump arms, it has to be said. I told myself her thighs must be something else altogether. I'd take her up the arse, I would. I forced myself to stay hard. At one point I was becoming less delirious, even at night. She'd wait until the gaslight had been dimmed to wish me goodnight, just to me. She said it nicely... She didn't cup my balls, though I was expecting it. Cos it was getting romantic. We was developing feelings. Even Bébert couldn't help noticing.

"If you want, when she bends over, you can fuck that bint from behind, all the way, but watch it, I'm warning yer, if an amputee shows up in this shithole, the wind'll blow in another direction and you'll be booted out before you can say knife. I ain't saying nothing, but consider yerself warned..."

He'd been around the block, Bébert. Unbelievable... Anyway. Another two weeks passed. We didn't go out. We didn't know what was going on outside, but our side must've retreated as the front was coming closer. That's to say, we could hear the big guns much better now, even from the room where we were lying, looking out on the courtyard. There was also enemy aeroplanes that had become a common sight around midday. Nothing too bad. Three bombs tops. The ladies would shriek and tremble and hide in the toilets. There is a special kind of bravery reserved for ladies. Méconille would simply clear off when it happened, running up the stairs and coming back down when it was over…

"There seem to be more and more of them," he'd say.

He was embarrassed.

My father wrote letters to me, perfectly written in a perfect style. He urged me to be patient, he predicted that there would be peace soon, he wrote to me about their difficulties, about their shop in the Passage des Bérésinas, the inexplicable meanness of their neighbours, the extra work he had to do at La Coccinelle to make up for the combatants.

"We have paid your canteen lady. Do not run up any more debts where you are; debts inexorably lead to dishonour."

He nevertheless complimented me fulsomely on my bravery. He seriously astonished me, though, with his talk of bravery. He had no idea what it was. Neither did I, mind you. In short, I was worried about him. Though I was drowning in this fucking mess – and it really was unbelievably awful – still I couldn't stop thinking about my father's letters because of their tone. Even with just ten minutes left to live, you'll search for the sweet remembrance of things past. My father's letters contained my whole bitch of a youth, which was dead and gone. I had no fond memories. It was all one stinking pile of horseshit, full of anxiety. Horrendous. And yet, it was my very own rotten childhood he sketched out in his army-censored postcards with their well-crafted, balanced sentences.

Being where I was, if I was going to croak, I'd've liked a more fitting music, something more me, more lively. The cruellest thing of the whole disgusting situation was that I didn't like the music of my father's prose. Had I died, I'd have risen from the dead to puke all over his prose. You can't remake yourself. Kicking the bucket isn't so hard, it's all the bollocks running up to it that drains the poetry out of you, the butchery, drivel and torture that precede your death rattle. You need to die young or be rich. When L'Espinasse came to fondle me at night, twice I nearly cried in her arms. I restrained myself. It was my father's fault, what with his cards. Because let me tell you one thing right now: I can be quite courageous on my own.

I bet you're dying to get to know the town of Peurdu-sur-la-Lys. It was another good three weeks before I was able to get up and was allowed out onto the streets. Anxiety-wise, I had my fill. I said nothing to Bébert. I think cos I felt he had his fair share of anxiety too. At the end of the day, my only protection was L'Espinasse. Méconille didn't count. She was the rich one, the one who paid for the upkeep of the hospital.

The padre dropped in every day. He was circling the carrion too, but it was easy to keep him happy. A confession every now and again and he was as pleased as Punch. He'd positively beam. I went to confession. Of course I didn't tell him anything, just trifles. I'm not that daft. Bébert too went to confession.

Méconille was of a more depraved sort. He insisted on extracting the bullet. Every morning he'd look inside my mouth and ear with optical instruments of all shapes and sizes, so much he ended up cross-eyed.

"You need to be brave, Ferdinand, and have it removed… Otherwise you'll lose your ear… and perhaps your head into the bargain…"

The thing to do was to play the idiot, to push back without irritating him too much. Seeing me battle it out with Méconille, Bébert nearly killed himself laughing. From the sideline L'Espinasse would encourage me to resist, but not too much. You'd think she was getting all wet watching me stand up to Méconille. At night she'd come to my bed and with a straight face she'd warm up my dick a good while. In the end, she was my only protection, even if, as Bébert pointed out, I shouldn't count on her all that much. Yeah, right! L'Espinasse rubbed shoulders with all the bigwigs on the general staff, and could, it seemed, recommend I get six months R&R and never be refused.

But there was more to come. One morning I saw a general with four stripes entering the ward, preceded by L'Espinasse, who else? Looking at their mugs, I could sense misfortune about to strike.

Ferdinand, I told myself, that's your enemy, your real, no-foolin' enemy, the enemy of your flesh and blood... Look at that general's mug. You may dodge him, but he'll catch you wherever you may hide, I told myself. I felt cut off from everyone. Right then, it was just my instinct talking, and it was bang on. They could offer me all they liked: sweet songs, funfairs, clotted cream, opera, bagpipes, even the silky arse of a heavenly angel.

I'm intelligent and obstinate as hell. If the Mont Blanc came trundling towards me on castors, I wouldn't budge. Your instinct is never wrong when it faces the ghastliness of man. The game was up. Time to count the bullets. Over and done with. The old codger came up to my bed. He sat down and opened his bulging briefcase. Bébert was listening in to see how I'd get out of this scrape. L'Espinasse introduced him.

"Ferdinand, this is Colonel Récumel, prosecutor for the court martial of the 92nd Army Corps. He is here to inquire into the circumstances in which you and your convoy fell. It was an ambush, wasn't it, Ferdinand, from what you've said before?… You were attacked by spies on the road, and at…"

She threw me a lifeline, the old bint. Handed me some ammo, as they say. Récumel's phiz was far from a pretty sight. I've seen a fair few mugs of NCOs that even a foraging rat would've thought twice about having a nibble at. But Colonel Récumel was more repulsive than anything I'd ever experienced. For starters, he had no cheeks. There were holes all over, like a corpse, and only a little bit of taut, yellow skin, hairy and translucent. Below the emptiness there couldn't be anything except pure malice. Deep in his hollow sockets, his eyes were so intense you forgot about the rest. Andalusian eyes burning with lust. A bald pate, gleaming in the white light. Just look at him, Ferdinand, I told myself again, even before he opens his mouth, you've reached the end of the road. There's surely no more frightening cunt in the whole of the French army. He's something else. If he can find a way, he'll have you shot tomorrow morning at dawn.

You should've heard the questions he asked me next. He had them all written down, but what I noticed from the outset, and which gave me some hope, was that he had no idea what he was talking about. It was all made up. With a bit more learning, I'd have cornered him there and then. He was talking out of his arse. I knew he was bullshitting, but I didn't have enough schooling to have him on. That would've made my comrades laugh. He didn't have the foggiest about what had happened to Le Drellière and the convoy. But he let on that he had. That's what made him such a stupid prick. You can't imagine things like that, especially not if you have a black heart. You sense it, and that's the end of it. Fuck all to explain, then. I let L'Espinasse do the talking. Like my father, she knew the art of talking loads without saying nothing. He didn't dare interrupt her. It was clear she was in charge and wielded power. I could've kissed her on the teeth. All the same, that gravedigger was after my hide. He went for me... what was left of me anyway. He fidgeted on his little iron chair, his arse shaking so much it sounded like a pair of castanets, that's how excited he was. But he was so far off with his insinuations that it was both funny and painful. I was nearly tempted to put him straight, to help him out. His blundering embarrassed me. He didn't have a clue about the War of Movement and the independent cavalry. They ought to send him to the dragoons for a good work-over. That would teach him. He might learn something, get the hang of things. In life, it's all about adopting the right tone, even for assassins.

"I can see, Corporal, that you have no recollection of the very precise orders that you were given or the content of a single one of the dispatches that were sent to you. I make it twelve in total" – he held them in his hand – "from the moment you left the railway station at... up to the moment where the events unfolded so rapidly, so inexplicably, four days later, when your convoy was completely annihilated by enemy artillery and forced to move beyond the Comtoise farmhouse, at exactly seven hundred metres from the river...

after yet another turnaround, following the great many variations of the [...] itinerary planned by your surviving superiors, changes that are inexplicable and frankly incredible given that at that point you were [...] at a distance of forty-two kilometres north of the main road. You should make at least another effort, given that you are at present the sole survivor of this grotesque saga... The sole survivor, that is, with a degree of lucidity, since cavalryman Krumenoy from the 2nd squadron, who was found in the vicinity of the hospital at Montluc, has not yet recovered his faculty of speech in these past two months."

I decided to have no more faculty of speech than Krumenoy. I kept my mouth shut. We had nothing in common. For starters, he talked all elegant, like my father. That was enough. In his bed, Bébert was quietly laughing his head off. The inquisitor turned around and stared daggers at him. It didn't bring him any luck, by the way. I'll get to that later... I thought to myself, if I don't say a word, what's he going to charge me with when it comes to it? Desertion in the face of the enemy? Abandoning my post? Something else nice?...

"All right," he said, finishing off. "I will investigate the matter." And he got up.

That bugger, I've never seen him again, but I've often thought about him. He had a funny old job. L'Espinasse had been my salvation. You was lucky, everyone around me kept saying. But in reality the bods in the beds around me were just jealous. Sickly, whining, bleeding bastards the lot of 'em. Ferdinand, I told myself, if the major drops the case, you must scram. Find yourself an alibi. Your good fortune causes envy...

I could clearly see that the wog corporal, the one with the missing eye, that he was getting less and less cautious, cos he was dying to bang the old bint.

Another two weeks passed. I was able to get up for longer. I could only hear with one ear, though. The other was like being inside a smithy, but never mind that. I wanted to go out. Bébert wanted to go out too, to see what was going on. Now it was two of us asking Miss L'Espinasse permission to go out! That night she returned to my bed again. The gaslight was dimmed, and there she was, L'Espinasse, at my bedside. I felt her breath on my nose. I knew it was a matter of life or death. I plucked up my courage. Now or never. I got hold of her mouth, her lips, and sucked on her teeth, in between her teeth and stroked her gums with the tip of my tongue. It tickled her. She was happy.

"Ferdinand," she whispered. "Ferdinand, do you like me a little, then?..."

We had to keep our voices down. The others were just pretending to snore. They were tossing themselves off. Outside it went *boom boom* all night long. There was continuous shelling about twenty kilometres away, maybe less. I kissed her arms for a change. I put two of her fingers in my mouth. I put her other hand on my dick. I wanted the slut to like me. I kissed her all over her mouth again. I'd've stuck my tongue up her arsehole, would've done anything, lap up her menstrual blood, as long as that geezer from the court martial would go and fuck himself. But my sweetie pie wasn't fooled.

"You were afraid just now, weren't you, Ferdinand? Of the colonel... The explanations you gave didn't make much sense..."

I didn't say a word. Didn't quite understand her... I just muttered something, cos I didn't know what else to do. She liked my being scared. She was getting off on it, the cow. She was rubbing herself up against the bed. She had a massive, Flemish rump. It was as if she'd made me crawl into her backside, and now she was climaxing, on her knees. It was a prayer.

"Tomorrow morning you should go to first mass, Ferdinand, and you will pray to God and give Him thanks for the protection He has given you and pray that you may get well. Good evening."

It was over. She had come and she was gone. The rest of the cripples were laughing their heads off. The whole thing felt like a cup-and-ball game. Twelve balls. Two balls. No balls... Bingo...

I waited for news the next morning. Nothing from the court martial. I casually tried to find out more from the bedridden guys who remembered being on campaign.

"Have you ever seen anyone get shot?" I asked the artillery man who had a piece of shrapnel in his lung and then another who had lost the tip of his tongue by the same means.

"I dhaw one dhied dho a pole in Thithonne. Dhey hott so badthy it dhook 'm free goes... Not fhunny."

That didn't really help.

"Horyunatewy an adjudhan," he added, "hott im free dhimes in da mouff."

Now *that* I could easily imagine. I wondered if they would take me to Romanches to execute me or if they'd do it right here in Peurdu. Anything was possible.

Inevitably I spent the night tormented by my infernal din, a fever and the prospect of being shot. I came *that* close to going to find L'Espinasse… Fuck it, though, I told myself I wouldn't lose, I didn't want to lose. Two more days, three more nights. Still nothing from the court martial. I reckoned they still hadn't discussed the regiment's cash box, which had been smashed as well and had vanished in the chaos, and yet it was the most serious thing they could pin on me, that bunch of scumbags, whose identity I wouldn't find out until the last moment. Even during my nightly fevers, though, I managed to prepare some truly moronic answers for them. Still nothing. I closely watched the breaking of the day – a grey, northern day, reflected in sparkling clean windows, appearing above pointed Flemish roofs gleaming with rain. I saw all that and I saw life return.

What with that gravedigger and Méconille, who was wondering if he was going to lose me before he could dig out my bullet, the army chaplain, who came twice a day to offer me eternity, and that bloody buzzing that made my whole carcass shake, I had a marvellous life, a life of torture, an ordeal that took away my sleep, or as good as. It was clear I would never again live like the others, like all those stupid bastards that take sleep and silence for granted, end of story. Three, four times at six in the morning I watched as the duty nurse opened the door. And then one morning, without us having been told, an Arab was brought in from the station. His leg had been shot to pieces by a howitzer, just above the knee.

"Watch that girl of yours," Bébert warned. "You're in for a larf."

43

And sure enough, from the moment the wog entered the Saint-Gonzef ward, she hardly looked at me. You should've seen her pant when she was near his bed, you'd think she'd swapped a bone for a leg of lamb. She lost no time in regaling the Arab with her biggest catheter, the one I knew well. He was moaning behind the screen. They were having us on. The very next morning, the doctor operated on him, a massive amputation from the thigh down. From that moment she wouldn't leave him alone. Let me put a catheter in you. You could almost say I was jealous. Bébert was taking the piss out of me. How about another catheter? The wog was in a bad way. They put up a screen around him. Bébert then told me what was going on. I refused to believe him, though I'd seen a thing or two. Bébert's fucking with me, I told myself. So I had to get out of bed, just to check. Méconille never saw a thing. Of Bébert and me, I mean. The others didn't have a clue anyway. The Arab didn't last long behind his screen. Two days later he was in such an awful state they took him down to the morgue.

He must have been wanked off at least ten times on his last day alone, and catheterised to boot, and not for laughs neither, by the director herself, behind the screen. And now he was dead and they were taking him to the basement. I could've kicked up a stink with what I knew, but that wouldn't've done me no good. Since I was able to get out of bed and I could walk to the end of the room, I plucked up my courage. I looked L'Espinasse straight in the eye.

"Can I not go out into town today after lunch?" I asked.

"But Ferdinand, how could you even think about it? You can hardly stand up."

"That's all right," I said. "Bébert will support me if I keel over."

I had some cheek asking her that. What with a court martial hanging over me, I shouldn't be allowed out at all. They could come for me any minute.

Being allowed to leave the sick house was exceptional, a favour. I shouldn't lose my nerve.

I said what I said…

"I'll be away for an hour or five."

She looked me up and down. She pulled her lips tight around her teeth. She's going to bite me, I thought. Not at all.

"It's all right, Ferdinand, but you need to take Bébert with you, and you must stay away from the main road, where you will almost certainly run into soldiers of the garrison, and I will no doubt get the blame, and you will go straight to prison. I'm warning you."

I didn't even say thanks.

"Bébert! At two o'clock we're off. But the others mustn't suspect we're going for a wander. We'll tell them buggers on the ward we're going to a specialist, and that you have to come with, on account of my arm."

"You're on!" he said, and we started shouting that a special specialist had come just to see me and that we were going to visit him at the other end of town.

They're sly bastards, though, them injured. Yet they seemed to swallow our porky pies. Great. At two o'clock we were out on the street. It was a narrow alley. But the fresh air did us good.

"Winter's over, Bébert," I told him. "Soon there'll be hope! When spring arrives, my skull's going to be buzzing more than ever. I'll let you know."

Bébert was always on the qui vive too. We had to avoid running into top brass. On his slippers he walked noiselessly from one door to the next, taking shelter every now and again. We looked at the gardens and the trees sticking out over the low brick walls. In the sky there were puffs of exploding shells and puffs of cloud too, pink and pale. The *poilus* we saw wore different uniforms from ours, all of the same colour and less ceremonial.* Fashion had already changed since we entered the Virginal Secours. Time flies. The fresh air made me a little dizzy, but with Bébert to lean on, I made good progress. Walking out on the street gave me a tremendous fucking wanderlust. I felt alive. It reminded me of the time I was peddling carved bracelets along the boulevards for some shop, which didn't end so well.* But I mustn't dwell on my memories, it would only spoil my day. It's incredible how few pleasant memories I have.

Peurdu-sur-la-Lys was a hoot. For us, at least. The central square all lined with pretty houses of finely carved stone, just like a museum. In the middle, market stalls selling carrots, turnips and salt meat. A sight for sore eyes. And trucks making the whole place shake –houses, markets, tootsies, and pongos from all kinds of armies manning their guns, hands in their pockets, under the arcades, cawing in little groups in the corners, dressed in yellow and green, Sidis and even Indians, masses of 'em, and a whole armada of cars... All that was swirling and shaking [...] like in a circus. It was the heart of the town; from there, the artillery shells, carrots and men would disperse in all directions.

Others were coming back from the front looking devastated, parading reluctantly, creating a line of mud that contrasted with the garish dragoons on the square. Bébert and me, we enjoyed the spectacle. Afterwards we plonked ourselves down in a little boozer and looked out of the window, taking it all in bit by bit.

Bébert wasn't great to look at. He didn't inspire confidence when you first met him, but essentially he was a decent guy.

The first drinks were on him. He had some money.

"My missus is doing well," he told me. "Working her arse off. I don't like being hard up…"

I got his drift. I'm not daft.

In this town everyone and his dog seemed to cross the main square.

"I'm sure," I said to Bébert, "that if we sit here long enough, we'll see Colonel Récumel walk past…"

"Forget about him," he replied. "Check out that waitress instead…"

It's true she was stacked… but two squaddies from the colonial troops were already fondling her tits, one each.

"She seems in good hands," I replied.

"My Angèle is twice as cute as that and everything else, you'll see. This one was scraped off the edge of a latrine," he said loudly so she'd hear him. "No way would I want her to polish my dick."

To show me he meant it, he spat on her shoes, a massive gob. She turned to look at him, giving him a good stare while he continued to look her up and down with disgust.

47

Suddenly she broke into a big smile. She ditched the two sergeants and walked towards him, looking all bashful and under his spell.

"Watch it, you slag, you're about to walk all over my foot. Bring me two glasses of *picon* and clear off. I may use her as my back-up bitch, that dirty slut, but first I've got to see my Angèle…"

He went into a sulk behind the half-curtain from where we were looking at the market square. He didn't even look at the waitress, as if she didn't exist. This in spite of her seeming to try and get him to spit on her once more. But he wasn't interested. He was thinking.

I let him think. I was mulling things over myself too. I was trying to keep abreast.

"You see," he said after a while, "it's teeming with Tommies here!… I'm going to write to Angèle… Now that I can go out, I'll get my arse in gear… I just hope my hoof will continue to fester for another two, three months. You's gonna have a good time with Angèle, Ferdinand. You'll even be able to send money orders to your folks… I'll pass her on to you, that waitress, I'll break her in for yer… It's the best I can do… I'll find another floozie… I don't believe in tarts like L'Espinasse… She can't be trusted. So, she's a sadist, so what? But one day she'll turn against you. You can't follow them. Whereas with Angèle, I know what I'm dealing with. You'll see what she brings in… She's a first-rate hunting dog… Ever seen a hunt?…"

Sure, I'd seen a hunt, but I'd rather not talk about it. Anyway, we had a good time. The *picon* went to Bébert's head, though. He started to brag and talk rubbish. That was his weakness. He had two, then a third. The waitress didn't want him to pay the last two rounds. They were on her.

"Stop treading on my foot, you slut," was all he could say to thank her.

Instead he just pinched her arse under her dress, but really hard and everywhere, making her grimace, and for so long, she turned pale. We got up and left.

"Don't turn around," Bébert told me.

I was beginning to be able to stand up straight. The boozer was full of civilians as well as servicemen and a fair few plain-clothes coppers among them too, no doubt. All sorts of tradesmen, farmers, Belgian grenadiers, and British sailors. It had a big pianola too, banging out music with its machine-gun cymbals. Together with the artillery shells exploding in the sky, it created a fabulous effect. That was the first time I heard 'Tipperary'.* It was getting dark. On our way back we stayed close to the houses. Not too fast. Neither of us was capable of that.

"If my foot festers for only two more months, Ferdinand," Bébert continued, "just two more months, with Angèle alone, just with her, you understand, I can make a killing…"

Now you're talking. Except we had to make sure they didn't see us. In principle no one was allowed out on the street. While we were hiding, some coppers on patrol passed by, and then a whole squadron of gendarmes, and after that some guys from the English military police with their truncheons and armbands. Thankfully we were saved by a detachment of military engineers. Without them I think we'd've been stuffed. They were pontoniers transporting their boats upside down on gun carriages. It was quite a bazaar with rattling chains, old bangers and clanking pots. All we had to do was merge with their outfit. We would be just two more instruments. So there we were, hobbling along as part of the swarm that was thankfully moving in the direction of our street. We peeled off when we got to our block. In three swings we reached the corner of the Virginal Secours, where a small door led down to the morgue. I didn't fancy passing through there.

"Never mind that," Bébert said. "But let's not enter together. I'll go through the garden. I can't go down the stairs, what with my foot. You go through the basement."

So I opened the gate. I didn't make a noise. I pushed it open very quietly. It creaked a bit regardless. I stood still and peered into the dark. There was another door further down, a strip of light underneath. I got closer. Quietly, so as not to be heard. I never know how much noise I make or don't make when I move about, on account of the ringing in my ears. I got closer all the same. I could hear the squeaking sound of a nail being extracted from a plank, and then the creaking of wood being forced... I told myself, they're putting the lid on a coffin in there. It must be the Sidi they're putting away. Tomorrow he'll be buried. They don't waste a minute. They were no doubt in a hurry to get rid of the Sidi because of the gangrene that you could smell right through the phenol. In the morgue, lying on stretchers, there were others who'd be next and didn't smell as bad. Where I was standing, behind the door, I could hear someone muttering. It wasn't the voice of fat Émilien, the cabinetmaker, who was known by everyone in the hospital and who, for obvious reasons, was always a bit drunk and sounded it as well. It was a prayer, in Latin. Maybe a nun who'd come down to say a rosary while they were at it?

I was intrigued. I stood there wondering what to do. If I didn't have a look, I'd never know. All I needed to do was to pull myself up on the partition wall and peek into the little room. I looked for a ladder or something and finally got onto some empty boxes. Someone must have heard me... I looked. At that moment I heard echoes of artillery that shook the windows and reverberated all over the basement. I had another look. I had to keep my cool. It was funny, I didn't want to say it, but I had a hunch. It was the voice of L'Espinasse I'd thought I'd heard praying in Latin. And now she was fully engaged in her task. The way she tried to open the coffin, you'd've thought everything she held dear was inside it. With a chisel she was trying to prise open the coffin. That's what was making the squeaking noise. Émilien had already nailed the lid on.

She was using both hands and was getting hurt. I couldn't see her face very well by the candlelight, also because she was wearing a veil and was bending down over the lid. She didn't care about the pong. But I did. I'm not sure I quite understood why, but suddenly I realized this was an intimate moment, real intimate. I made the most of it. I knocked on the partition wall. She looked up. She could clearly see me by the light of her candle, not two metres away from her.

But then she scared me. I stepped back a little. That was not a grimace on her face, it was more like a big, pale wound, slavering and trembling.

"Bleed from your gob," I told her. "Bleed, you disgusting sow!"

I insulted her cos I didn't know what else to say. And it came from deep down – it wasn't the moment to talk sense. I clambered down, stumbling, and pushed open the door to the little room.

"Bleed, you filthy sow, bleed!"

It was a stupid thing to say, but I couldn't think of anything else. Then she pounced on me, and with her whole face started to kiss me all over, sucking at me as if was dead too. She held me with both her arms, her whole body shaking. Then she became heavy and suddenly she let go and slipped onto the ground. I caught her.

She nearly fainted.

"Aline," I said. "Aline!"

That was her first name, I'd heard them use it on the ward. In the darkness she slowly got to her feet.

"I'm going back up," I said.

"That's right, Ferdinand. I'll see you tomorrow. Until then. I'm feeling better now. You're kind, Ferdinand. I'm so fond of you..."

She went out onto the street. She was almost her old self. But upstairs Bébert was getting worried.

"I thought you got yerself nabbed by the caretaker," he said.

He smelt a rat. I wasn't going to tell him what had happened. Not to him, not to no one. People need to be strong so as not to do harm. Plus I could use it to my advantage, and I did.

I didn't really believe in new days. Each morning I was more tired than when I went to bed, cos in the course of the night I'd be woken up twenty, thirty times by the ringing in my ears. It was a nameless kind of tiredness, the kind you get from anguish. Everyone knows what you need to do: you need to sleep to go back to being a man like the others again. You get too tired even to feel the urge to kill yourself. Everything becomes tiredness. Every morning, when they changed his dressing, Cascade* was happy. His foot wasn't getting any better. He'd soon lose two more phalanxes due to bone caries. He shouldn't've been walking, not even on slippers. But his situation also earned him special privileges from Miss L'Espinasse, though what exactly they were, he never told me... After all, he was cautious too.

"So what's your name, then, nice tits?" he asked the waitress the second time we went back.

"Amandine Destinée Vandercotte."

"Ain't that a pretty name?" replied Cascade, as if he was delighted. "Been working here long?"

"Two years."

"So you got to know the town well, then? And the people! Do you happen to know L'Espinasse? Tell me, you eat pussy?"

"I do," she replied. "You?"

"I'll let you know after I've given you a right royal kick up the arse and not a moment sooner, you slut! These kids, sticking their noses in and then getting all timid on me. Asking questions…"

He pretended to be unhappy, insulted. He was laying it on thick to impress me. It's true he had no trouble with Amandine. She'd never seen anything so impressive.

We went back every day after lunch at noon. It was called the Café de l'Hyperbole, on the Place Majeure. We had our corner, our own table. We could see everything. And no one could see us. Us leaving the Virginal Secours stirred up a bit of envy. L'Espinasse had made us promise we'd tell those tossers on the ward that we were allowed out every day for some electrical treatment.

"Sure thing!" I told L'Espinasse, that old girl.

I was learning how to talk proper, like Bébert. But I kept my secret. Even Bébert I didn't trust. He had a curious way of operating in life. Never made any noise. He would normally talk with his hand in front of his mouth, except when he was shouting at Destinée Amandine, who chuckled with pleasure when he called her such savage names as she'd never heard before. He'd also pinch her buttocks on the sly and real hard too as she trotted to the bar and back. A harsh one, this Bébert. For at least eight days we came back and ensconced ourselves behind the half-curtain at L'Hyperbole. Bébert spied out the whole square, the movement of the troops, the people, the officers. He was learning to distinguish between the uniforms of all the different armies. Amandine Destinée helped him.

"That thing there on the corner, that kind of castle, that's the headquarters of the English general staff. Them what wear red bands around their caps are the richest."

She knew on account of the tips.

I'd listen to Cascade from the crack of dawn. He'd tell me about Angèle, that she had mahogany hair falling down to her hips. Orgasm-wise, she could come twelve times in a row. It was beautiful. She would swoon. And her blowjobs were out of this world, God's honest truth...

"You'll see!"

Bébert wasn't obsessed or anything. These things hadn't messed with his mind. I tried to get back on track. Just had to. Life's even more unbearable if you can't even get it up. It's just wrong.

"Tell me a little more about Angèle," I asked him quietly, so as not to wake anyone up.

He told me how he took her up the arse for the first time, up her bunghole, and how it had hurt at first and how she'd screamed for about an hour.

In the morning, the Zouave to my left would look so incredibly pale in the early daylight that each time I thought he was dead. But then he'd stir and start his groaning all over again. It took him two months to die...

I tried to track down L'Espinasse to find out who she was jerking off this time, but there was so many wounded soldiers arriving, a couple of jam-packed carriages various times a day, that I got lost. Peurdu-sur-la-Lys was an intense place.

They said there was at least four general staffs and twelve hospitals, three field hospitals, two courts martial and twenty artillery parks between the Place Majeur and the second series of ramparts. In the seminary reservists were quartered from eleven villages in the area. Miss L'Espinasse also did her best to do a bit of good to those poor devils, as she called them.

It was in a walled garden behind the seminary at the break of day that executions took place. A volley and then a second one a quarter of an hour later. About twice a week. From the Saint-Gonzef ward I'd more or less established the frequency. It was nearly always on a Wednesday and a Friday. Thursday was market day, a different kind of noise. Cascade was aware too. He didn't really like to talk about it. But I suspected he actually really wanted to go there. Just to check the place out. So did I. It was crucial to go there alone. And we always went out together. Until one day we surprised each other in a comical way. There was some errand to run. Picking up meds at the station. I said I couldn't go, cos it was too far and too heavy to carry and someone always had to stop me from keeling over on the way. So Cascade went by himself. But I looked at his face, and there was something off about the way he looked. He was cooking something up.

"I'm not going," I told him.

But when he turned his back to get his shoes on, I nicked the chit from his greatcoat draped over the chair. He left. I waited five minutes and then I started to shout to get the staff's attention.

"Look, he forgot his chit. He'll never get his parcel now."

And I ran after him, supposedly to catch him up.

Great, I told myself once I was out on the street. This gives me a chance to see what it's like behind the seminary...

I took care not to bump into the pigs. I got to the exact spot where you entered something like a cul-de-sac. At the end there was a wrought-iron door that led to a walled garden. I walked over to it. I stooped and put my eye to the keyhole. What I saw was a kind of garden with a lawn and a wall at the far end, about one hundred metres away at least, a burrstone wall, not very high. What do they tie them to? It was difficult to imagine exactly. But you could sort of get the picture. I'd've liked to have seen bullet holes. It was very quiet. Nearby it was spring with birds singing. They were whistling like bullets, them birds. They must put up a new post each time. I needed to get to the station. I left. I bumped into Cascade just around the corner. He must've dawdled on his way to the station. We didn't say a thing. He looked shaken. We're all as brave as we can be. I gave him his chit back.

"Go and get that parcel of theirs," I told him.

"Come with," he suggested.

It was me this time who nearly had to support him to the collection point. Later I realized he'd had a premonition as soon as he saw me. On the way back we stopped at L'Hyperbole. He was quiet. Not a dicky bird to Destinée Amandine, nothing. It made her cry. We drank a whole litre of curaçao. I'm sure Cascade didn't sleep a wink that night. The next morning a strange sort of knowing air had come over him. Don't go thinking Bébert had no feelings. The proof is that he knew how to stay silent, for hours on end, thinking about this and that, staring into space. He had quite a nice mug, as far as I can judge men, with fine and regular traits and rather big eyes, like an idealist. But while waiting to hit the big time he was really quite harsh on them floozies, though they knew he was right, that he was correct and spoke the truth. He took me for a gobshite, a friendly but lazy sod, corrupted by too much regular work. I'd told him everything, nearly everything. The only thing I kept for myself was that stuff about L'Espinasse, which remained a deep secret, tied up with the very life of me, so to speak.

Meanwhile, there was no more talk of Colonel Récumel from the court martial. All we had was the walled garden where it took place and where Cascade had his premonition. He must not have gathered enough evidence against me about the affair. I often thought I heard him speak to me, but it was only a few delirious words that came to me in the evening when I still came down with a fever. I didn't say anything about it, so they wouldn't stop me from going out. L'Espinasse no longer wanked me off. She just came to kiss me goodnight around ten o'clock. She seemed to have calmed down a little. The padre avoided talking to me for now. He must've suspected something. That quack Méconille had become more polite too. Bébert noticed the changes around us as well, but he didn't really get what it was all about. Didn't stop him from studying the customs of war in town, though. As I've told you, in the dark corners of L'Hyperbole there was always a tremendous hullaballoo, and that's not even counting the pianola. When everyone was shouting at each other, it created a kind of silence in my ear. Noise against noise. Except it made me feel faint. Too much conflict in the old nut, no doubt.

"Come, Ferdinand," Bébert would say to me. "You look all pale. Come, we'll go for a walk along the river. That'll do you some good."

We'd hobble there. We'd watch the artillery shells explode in the distant sky. Behind the poplars spring had come back. Then we'd return to L'Hyperbole, where he'd continue his observations. Watching the troops parade was like something out of a picture book [...]. It was busiest at around eight in the evening at the changeover.

Then the regiments would stream onto the Place Majeure like flows of lava, from one end to the other, left to right. They'd flood the arcades surrounding the market area, lapping up against the bistros, past the fountain, guzzling up entire troughs, with big garlands of lanterns swaying between the axles of their vehicles.* All that would've finally melted into one on the Place Majeure. They just needed to pound the flesh and other material a little. This actually happened too, they told me. One day, on the night of 24th November,* the Bavarians shelled the whole place to smithereens during a barrage.

Then everything stopped gravitating towards the Place Majeure. The Belgian divisions returned to the bowels of Zeeland when suddenly forty-three artillery shells landed on top of them. Ten dead.

Three colonels were killed playing poker, in the priest's garden no less. I can't guarantee any of that, since I didn't see it, but that's what they've told me. It was still as flashy and rowdy as always over at L'Hyperbole, where Cascade and me would spend the afternoon. In Peurdu-sur-la-Lys squaddies were dropped off and picked up at the Place Majeure, and you've got to admit, the saddest thing for those who only had a few hours to spend was not the lack of drink – there was plenty of that around – no, it was women. Amandine Destinée was the only barmaid we knew well, and she only had eyes for Cascade, that much was clear. It was love at first sight. As for all the other randy buggers, whether they came to her from Ypres, heroic Liège or Alaska, she couldn't even stand the way they smelt. There were no cat houses. They were forbidden by all the regulations, and the clandestine hookers were hunted down, locked up or kicked out by all four police forces.

So after a drink and a snooze everyone'd just toss them-selves off or fuck each other up the arse, some of the Allies at least, cos at the time that kind of scenario was not yet widespread among us. All in all, from Cascade's point of view, there was a lot of money up for grabs all around us. Angèle just had to come over, that was his opinion. I pushed back, I have to say, to my credit. I pushed back hard because fate was already menacing and threatening enough. Cascade could be married matrimonially to her all he liked, with papers signed by the Republic and everything, but if they ever caught Angèle being banged at the going exchange rate, he would not be spared, never mind his rotting foot, and sent straight to the 70th regiment to have that ugly head of his rearranged at the front line in less than no time, or even quicker... Anyway, I'd rather not talk about premonitions. We understood each other. It was no good. I'd have said Cascade was fixated, hell-bent even, on his own perdition. He wouldn't stop until Angèle had her permit. And lo and behold, his Angèle rocked up one morning unannounced in the Saint-Gonzef ward. He hadn't lied: she was smoking hot. With one look she would set your dick on fire, with one gesture. It went even deeper than that, right to the heart, so to speak, or deeper still, to the very essence of you, which is no longer at any depth at all, since it's only separated from death by three quivering slivers of life, but quivering so much, so intensely, so vigorously that the only thing you can say is yes, yes!

From where we found ourselves, me above all compared with the others, at the bottom of a vat of pain, for me to climb out of it, I needed a ladder, like the one held out by Angèle and her anatomy. She was coming on to me big time right from the get-go, encouraging me. It didn't bother Cascade.

"You see, Ferdinand. I didn't lie to you. Check out her bum when she leaves. And when she goes to see them squaddies, she's bound to provoke a mutiny. I told you, she's hot as hell... Go on, my girl. Go and look for the arcades... the Café de l'Hyperbole. Ask for Destinée, the waitress. I've given her a heads-up. She'll put you up... I'll come and get you this afternoon with my mate. Go and get your permit signed at the constabulary... Don't go out until I tell you... I've got it all planned... Sort yourself out... Don't talk to no one... If they ask questions, cry a little, say your hubby's very ill... And it's true too. Anyway, you get my drift... Now beat it..."

I couldn't get over Angèle, I'd gone completely gaga. I'd've licked the inside of her thighs there and then. I'd've paid any sum, had I had the wherewithal. Cascade was looking at me. He thought it was funny.

"Don't get overexcited, Loulou.* If you's still my mate when you're able to get it up again, I'll let you screw that cute little tart and I'll tell her to squirm and come as if you was an officer. You couldn't arsk for nothing more..."

That summer, short, thin blouses were in fashion. I thought of hers, conjuring up a dreamlike veil with her nipples showing through, which unleashed a massive buzzing thunderstorm in my head. I had to go to the crapper to puke because of the dizziness that knocked me sideways when I got overexcited.

We went out as usual. Destinée was at L'Hyperbole, surrounded as always by soldiers. Angèle was there too, drinking anisette with some Senegalese. Cascade was not amused and told me:

"Since it's the first time, I don't want to embarrass her in front of my back-up bitch, but if she starts hanging around men left and right, I'll prick her in the fat of the arse... I'll teach her to be promiscuous. Say, wifey," he said to her, "you've developed some funny habits since I got injured... Listen, you're not in Paris. I'm right here... You'll go where I tell you to go and nowhere else..."

Angèle was not best pleased with his remarks, that much was obvious. I was embarrassed for her. It was true she seemed a bit tense.

"You see, Ferdinand ain't going to have a good opinion of you, and goodness knows I've sung your praises, just ask him. Show him your twat. Come on, show Ferdinand your twat, I'm telling you!..."

Angèle wasn't happy, not a bit. She refused. In cases like that, he'd get pretty violent.

"Show him! If not, I'll smack you across your fucking face with my crutch!"

Destinée was standing behind Cascade. She didn't know how to react, but she trembled with fear for Angèle.

But Angèle didn't give an inch. He thought better of it on account of the scandal it would've provoked. Angèle gave him a long, hard look. He gave in. There was the whole war too that had crushed us. Cascade could no longer beat the living daylights out of his missus. Angèle stared him up and down for a full minute.

"You stink, Cascade," she said. "You stink and you can kiss my arse. I've come here just to tell you straight to your face. Plus, I can get you kicked out whenever I feel like…"

That hit him right in the kisser. It must have been the first time anyone called him a shit in front of others, and his very own wife no less…

"Shht," he whispered. "Shht!" he said again. "You've had too much to drink, Angèle. If you repeat anything you've just said, I'll fucking kill you soon as we leave this place…"

He was back in control.

This all took place in a small room at the back, but she screamed so loud I got scared. She continued to fill me in, in a whisper this time, saying it was all for show. He was all shook up. You could see why. In the end we had a few drinks, paid for by her. She sneered at seeing him so fearful.

"Scared the bejesus out of yer, didn't I, Cascade? You're in my clutches now… I'm sick of that ugly mug of yours…"

"You're heartless, Angèle. You're heartless," he said.

He rolled his eyes so you could only see the white. He was scared. He left L'Hyperbole to go back to the sick house just as a patrol passed by. In spite of that, she slipped us a hundred-franc note, and then, in front of Destinée, she told us:

"And don't fight, you two. Tomorrow I'll be the one in charge," she added.

All of that stuff is hardly important, because in the end it got mixed up with all sorts of horrors and diseases. I'm reporting it because I find it amusing. Cascade, though, was terrified.

"I never believed she'd turn out like that, Ferdinand... It's them foreigners what's ruining her."

That's how he saw it. He went to bed thinking about it. And in the morning he was still banging on about it.

Back at L'Hyperbole Angèle no doubt corrupted Destinée. They shared a room together. And then she started to have even more diabolical ideas.

I had such bad headaches I couldn't go out every day. It annoyed me. In the beginning I was in too much pain to get involved with her. L'Espinasse was keeping an eye on me. She no longer kissed me goodnight. She no longer spoke to me. The Zouave next to me died. One evening, when I got back, he was gone. That night was worse than usual. I'd got used to the Zouave, to his disgusting belly, the lot. I was convinced that his departure was a sign of worse to come. Only the worst could happen now.

But as you'll see, I got it wrong. Cascade and me were distrustful of what Angèle got up to in town with her residence permit. He might have been her pimp and all, he no longer had any control over her.

"You have no idea what a woman can do in her position. They're like panthers let out of their cage, knowing neither friend nor foe... Asking her to come here was the stupidest thing I've ever done in my life. I thought like I did before... I saw her as before... I don't know what they've done to her..."

He knew.

"I'm sure she hops into bed with everyone and his dog. She's going to get caught, and then I'm sure she'll rat me out... Cos let me tell you, she's become a real snake in the grass... That's how they sent her to me from Paris, in spite of my giving my sister clear instructions before I left. Unbe-fucking-lievable. If I ever find out, I'll offer them rozzers a bedside rug, you hear, a bedside rug made from the flayed skin of her arse. I'll give her a thrashing she's unlikely to ever forget before I dump her."

With his two hands he sketched an imaginary rug at my feet.

All the other guys except the dying were laughing their heads off hearing him rail against his missus. Other than that, they didn't give a toss about Cascade's stories. They didn't get them and preferred to play cards more than anything, and to spit and to squeeze droplets of piss into a urinal, waiting for the home front to write to them, telling them everything was hunky dory and there'd be peace soon. Around 15th July the big guns moved ever closer, which was a real nuisance. On the ward we often had to raise our voices and well-nigh shout to be heard and repeat the cards. During the day, the sky got so hot, you still saw red after you closed your eyelids.

Fortunately our little street was calm. Turning right, about two minutes away, the Lys flowed. We'd follow the towpath for a bit and arrived at the other side of the ramparts. From there you could look out over the countryside, that's to say, the fields on the side where there was peace. And on this peaceful side, sheep were grazing on green pasture. Cascade and me watched them munching flowers. We sat down. We barely heard the big guns. The water was calm, there were no barges any more. The wind was blowing in the poplar trees in short gusts that sounded like little laughs. The only annoying thing was them birds with their cries that sounded just like whistling bullets. We didn't say much. Having met Angèle, I told myself Cascade was in at least as much danger as me.

The towpath wasn't used by troops. All inland navigation had been halted. The water was black and still, with water lilies floating on it. The sun was rolling in the sky, but would sometimes just go and hide in the blackness, for no good reason. A sensitive fellow. I was beginning to put some order into the ringing in my ears. Trombones on one side, the organ only if I closed my eyes, the big drum with every heartbeat. If I hadn't suffered from vertigo and nausea so much, I'd've got used to it. But as it was, falling asleep at night was hard. For that you need to be happy, relaxed, able to give yourself over. It was no longer something I could hope to achieve. Compared to me, what Cascade had was nothing. I'd have gladly allowed both of my feet to rot away if that would leave my head in peace. He didn't get it. You never understand other people's obsessions. Peaceful fields don't mean shit to someone whose ears are full of noise.

You're better off being a proper musician. Would it take your mind off things if you had a passion like L'Espinasse? Or if you was a Chinaman, perhaps, consoling yourself with torturing people.

I had to find something like that too, something crazy, to make up for the misery of being forever locked up inside my head. I could never sit around and be idle any more with this thing going on all the time. I couldn't even say if I was mad or not. If I only had a little temperature, weird stuff would start happening to me. I no longer got enough sleep to have clear thoughts that meant something to me. I didn't care about any of 'em. In a sense, that's what saved me, if I may say so, cos otherwise I'd've made an end to it there and then. I wouldn't have waited long. I'd've let Méconille do his thing.

"It's soothing, the countryside," Cascade said, looking out over the fields. "It's soothing and treacherous at the same time on account of them cows. It was in the Bois that I found my real name. My name ain't Cascade, really, and I ain't called Gontran neither. My name is Julien Boisson."

He handed over the information like it was a confession. And then we left. Something was eating him. On the way back, we tried to avoid the alleyway that led to the garden where the executions took place. We chose quieter streets lined with convents. But that didn't calm our consciences neither. It was too tranquil. We changed course and put ourselves into the hands of fate by walking in the middle of the road.

"Let's see what she's up to," he said.

We hadn't dared return to L'Hyperbole for the past three days. So we entered the street with the town hall and then the one with the monumental staircase that fans out onto the middle of the central square. There we halted. We spied out the place before crossing the square. We always had to be on the lookout for coppers, seeing as our outings were not exactly legit. The Belgians in particular were real arseholes. Of all the police forces, they were the meanest bastards. They were cunning and sly and knew all the places where two or three races cross.

On the Place Majeure, there was a real hustle and bustle, the usual chaos as well as the awnings of the market stalls. There was a market every day now, because there was so much trade. A bit towards the left, there was the most beautiful building of them all, at least three floors of carved stone. It housed the British general staff. You should've seen the cars and the well-dressed guys coming out of there. It appeared the Prince of Wales was there every weekend. They also said the Kronprinz had come to see him to ask if they could stop the shelling for three hours on a Sunday, so they could bury the dead. Would you believe it?

And who do you reckon we see? Less than twenty metres from an English sentry? All dolled out in crape? We had no trouble recognizing her, though. Cascade stopped for a minute. To think. He got the picture.

"You see, Ferdinand, she's hustling... She's touting for English punters, I'm telling you..."

I'm no expert, but that's exactly what Angèle appeared to be doing at that moment. Cascade was still thinking.

"If you butt in on her now, worked up as she is, you can expect her to do anything, Cascade! I'm off…"

"Stay. We're going to handle this with kid gloves. Or rather, don't tell her I'm here. Go over there yourself and tell her any old story."

It worked out pretty OK. She was having a whale of a time. The evening before she'd had three officers already, and nothing but Englishmen.

"They're real generous. I make 'em feel sorry for me."

That explained the veil. She claimed she'd already lost her poor father at the Somme and that her husband was in hospital here in Peurdu-sur-la-Lys. Her husband was called Gontran Cascade, and she had her false permit to prove it. So it was all above board. The British officers would pay for a French lesson with her, with a bit of feeling thrown in. The previous evening alone she'd made twelve pounds.

"And you didn't steal nothing?" I asked.

"No, nothing, I swear, they get off on my bad luck."

She was having a great time with me, and I made use of the situation to grope her a little.

Cascade was waiting for us at L'Hyperbole. That's what we'd agreed if I could get it done. And I did. I can't say I seduced Angèle, but she put up with me more than with her hubby. She couldn't stand the would-be back-up bitch, the barmaid Destinée, even though they still shared a room.

"Say," she told Cascade almost immediately, "could you not teach your whore to wash her gash before going to bed?"

I thought he would chuck his beer bottle in her face, but his manhood had already checked out. Bébert was already on his way to meet his fate, and you'd've thought he knew it.

"It won't bring you any luck, Angèle, what you're doing. It won't bring you any luck. Just remember. Ever since I left Paris you've got too big for your boots. You don't have the brains to play the man, Angèle. It'll go to your head, it'll be your undoing, more even than mine... Just remember."

He spoke to her softly. He surprised me.

Before we left, she gave him another one-hundred-franc note in front of everyone. There was enough for the two of us. I wouldn't ask my parents for no more money. And then we saw them again, my parents, we saw everything again and everyone, all in one go. It was like a violent gust of wind from times past. I'll explain what happened. One Sunday, L'Espinasse barged into the ward with an enormous smile, and she directed all her attention to me. At first, I was suspicious, as I was having a wee wank underneath my bolster.

"Ferdinand," she told me. "Can you guess what great news I bring?"

That's it, I told myself. I've been declared unfit for service, just like that, without them even examining me.

"No? You have just been awarded the *médaille militaire* by Marshal Joffre."*

At that point I came out of my hiding place.

"Your dear parents will be here tomorrow. They have been informed too. Here is your magnificent citation..."

She read it out loud so everyone would hear.

"Corporal Ferdinand has been cited in the General Orders of the Army for having endeavoured single-handedly to relieve the convoy for which he was tasked with a mission of reconnaissance. The moment said convoy, having been surprised by artillery and attacked by enemy cavalry, found itself in difficulty, Corporal Ferdinand, unaided, attacked a group of Bavarian lancers three times, and thus, thanks to his bravery, succeeded in providing cover for the retreat of three hundred of the convoy's injured soldiers. In the course of this heroic act, Corporal Ferdinand sustained various wounds."

That was me. I told myself immediately: Ferdinand, there's got to be a mistake. It's the moment to make the most of it. I can't say I hesitated for even two minutes.

Such reversals never last. I don't know if there was a link, but that same day the front at Peurdu moved as well. They say the Germans retreated, a feigned retreat. We hardly heard the big guns any more. The other pongos on the ward couldn't get over my sudden promotion. To be honest, they were a bit jealous. Even Cascade was interested to some extent. I didn't tell him it was all made up, that stuff in my citation. He wouldn't have believed me.

I've got to admit that from then on everything became cushy and surreal. A great wind of imagination was blowing all around us. It gave me great courage, though, and I let myself be swept up in it all, it has to be said. I didn't give in to the surprise, or else I'd have stayed as stupid as before, putting up with misery and nothing but misery, cos that was all there was and all I'd ever known since my good parents raised me: a misery marked by no end of pain, toil and sweat. I could've chosen not to go along with the whole charade, that circus in which I was expected to mount a wooden charger, all decked out in lies and velvet. I could've refused. But I didn't.

Terrific, I said, there's a fine wind blowing, Ferdinand, rig out your galley, let the stupid bastards stew in their own shit, let yourself be pushed, stop believing in anything. Two out of three bits of you are kaput, but with what's left you're going to have a great time. Let yourself be blown along by this cold gale. Sleep or don't sleep, stagger, shag, reel, puke, froth, fester, shake, crush, betray, have no shame. It's the way the wind blows, and you'll never be as horrendous or raving mad as the rest of the world put together. Get ahead, that's all that's demanded of you. You've got your medal, you're handsome. In the battle of dickheads, you've finally got the upper hand. You've got your own special fanfare in your head, only half of you is eaten up by gangrene. You're rotting away, for sure, but you've seen battlefields, and it ain't rotting corpses that get decorated... and you, you've got a medal, don't you forget it, or else you're an ungrateful swine, a puddle of sick, a drivelling scumbag, not worth the paper they wipe your arse with.

Anyway, I stuck the citation with Joffre's signature in my pocket. I started to stick out my chest once again. My stroke of luck, it seemed, pushed Cascade further up shit creek. He even stopped moaning.

"Chin up, Gontran," I told him. "You'll see how I'm going to screw them old bags, L'Espinasse, the guys from the medical tribunal, the bishop. Boy, the way I feel now, I'll take him right up the arse if he won't talk to me when we stand at attention."

My jokes failed to cheer Cascade up.

"You're looking good, Ferdinand, real good," was all he could say. "You should have your picture taken."

"You bet I will."

I went to the photographer with my parents the very same afternoon they came up. My father was stunned. Suddenly I'd become someone. In the Passage des Bérésinas everyone was talking about my medal, they said. My mother shed a little tear, her voice choked. I found it quite revolting. I don't like it when my parents get emotional. We had bigger bones to pick. My father was impressed by the artillery units parading in the streets. My mother kept on saying how young the soldiers were and how imposing the officers looked on their horses. They inspired confidence. My father happened to have an acquaintance in Peurdu-sur-la-Lys, an insurance agent from La Coccinelle. We'd been invited for lunch to celebrate my medal. L'Espinasse had been invited too. I was the pride of her hospital. Cascade would be there as well, seeing as we were always together, and then my mother wanted Angèle to come along too, given that they were married. She didn't have a clue about the actual state of affairs. We couldn't really explain it either. They would leave the same evening. We went to look for Angèle and found her on the corner outside the English headquarters, as on the previous days.

Cascade was a total wreck, it has to be said. He melted away, especially when he saw Angèle. He stopped grumbling. Even Destinée was taking liberties. In L'Hyperbole she moved his chair back to avoid him blocking her clients' way. The man was transformed. Where I felt puffed up by my medal, something was eating him up inside. Something that came from the war, something he no longer understood. He'd lost his bluster, whereas I had grown, plus it seemed he'd resigned himself completely to his bad luck.

"Buck up," I told him. "You're under the spell of Angèle, and I agree, at the moment she's all hoity-toity. She's making the most of the situation we're in, but it won't last. You'll get her back when things take a nasty turn. She'll only be too happy for you to pull her up on her lying ways, and it wouldn't be a minute too late…"

"Man, man, man, I'm *that* close to handing her over to the pigs in person, I hardly recognize myself. For all I care, they can send her right back to Paris to be buggered by her niggers. It ain't about whether she stays or leaves, but whether I do *her* in or whether she will be the death of *me*. War only brings misery, say what you want. I'm sure she's got a lover boy somewhere, if she ain't a lezzer on top of it all, with me never suspecting a thing [...]. I swear, Ferdinand, Angèle's a monster."

The agent from La Coccinelle was called Mr Harnache. He lived in a pretty house, about as comfortable as you could get at the time. He was unbelievably friendly. He showed us the whole place from top to bottom. It was old school, and my mother was all over it. She was very complimentary. She felt sorry for Mr Harnache for having to live so close to the front. Their cute kids, two boys and a girl, joined us at the table. Mr Harnache was born into wealth and only looked after La Coccinelle to give himself something to do.

My mother's admiration for him knew no bounds. Here was a man who was the embodiment of courage and plenty of other virtues. So rich, [...] among the troops so near the front, with such lovely children around him, declared unfit for service on account of a weak heart, living in such a large and well-furnished home, all "old-school" with three maids and a cook, at less than twenty kilometres from the front, so easygoing with us, so attentive, receiving us at his table from day one, particularly unassuming towards Cascade, inquisitive, considerate, all but venerating our wounds and my military medal, dressed in a suit cut from really expensive cloth with a matching collar, very high and impeccable, well-connected with the cream of society of Peurdu-sur-la-Lys, knowing everyone and yet not in the least haughty, speaking

English like a textbook, his house decorated with filet-lace curtains, which my mother considered to be the ultimate proof of good taste, writing letters to my father almost as good as he wrote himself – not quite as good, obviously, but admirable nevertheless – and with a crew cut, already going out of fashion at the time, a no-nonsense haircut that makes one look so well groomed and perfectly masculine and proper, inspiring confidence in potential clients. My mother struggled to get up the stairs with her "gammy leg", as she called it,* but couldn't stop saying how wonderful everything was in the residence of Mr and Mrs Harnache.

She halted at the windows to catch her breath and looked out onto the street, where there was a coming and going of troops. She stayed there for a while, troubled by the carnivalesque spectacle…

"You can still hear the big guns," she commented.

And then she continued to the next room, where she admired the treasures inherited by many generations of Harnaches. Had you shown her a river full of fish instead of these troops in the street, my mother wouldn't have understood any more what possessed them to march one after the other in a torrent of colours. My father felt compelled to give her vague explanations, completely made up, pretending to be an expert. Harnache himself, amiable as he was, explained the formation of the Hindu troops…

"Moreover, they always walk in twos. Apparently, if one of the two comrades gets hit by an enemy bullet, the other hardly ever survives. It's a fact."

How this excited my mother! Finally something that plucked at her heartstrings.

"Look out where you put your foot when you step back, Célestine,"* my father said on account of the well-polished stairs of this exemplary house.

"A real museum… You have such beautiful things in your home, Madame…" my mother kept on congratulating her.

Mrs Harnache was waiting downstairs, at the entrance to the dining room, with her three children. My father was afraid my mother would trip up in front of everyone. She owed her limp to having walked up and down too many stairs, railroad tracks and pavements all over town. The thought of her pitiful stick leg made my father grimace. He was sure the others had seen it poking out from beneath her dress as she walked up the stairs. Harnache looked like a lewd pig with his little whiskers. I'm sure he felt up the maids. My father was ogling the maids as they were putting the hors d'oeuvres on the table. Sturdy, plump twenty-somethings. When they went to the kitchen to fetch the dishes, they had to go up two steps, offering us a glimpse of their calves.

Miss L'Espinasse arrived a little late and offered her profuse apologies. She'd been prevented from crossing the Place Majeure by a parade of Scots Guards who had disembarked the night before and whose general handed them over their flag.

"Oh, it was beautiful! Such strapping lads, Madame! Almost children still, true, but ravishingly fresh and brave and hardy!… I'm convinced that one day they will do marvellous deeds and give those vile Huns hell, those horrible animals!"

"To be sure, Madame, in the newspapers you can read all about their atrocious cruelty. It is beyond belief! There ought be a way of preventing those sorts of things from happening."

They spared Cascade and me the atrocities. They didn't want to reveal everything they'd read in the newspapers. As far as my mother was concerned, there ultimately had to be a way of appealing to someone very powerful to prevent the Germans from giving in to their every instinct. There simply had to be. For once, my father was in full agreement with her. Should the Germans be able to get away with all of this, the world would be different from what they'd always thought it to be, built on different principles, other notions, and what they thought had to remain the truth. And of course, there *was* a way to prevent the brutality of the war. All you had to do was do your duty to others, like my father had always done in his own life. That was all. They couldn't conceive of this world of atrocities, of never-ending torture. So they pretended it didn't exist. Merely imagining it as a possibility horrified them more than anything else. They tucked into their hors d'oeuvres, eating compulsively, getting red in the face, encouraging each other to deny there was anything that could be done against the atrocities of the Germans.

"It won't last. All we need is an American intervention."

Cascade and me, we could see that Miss L'Espinasse was a bit more hesitant in showing her indignation than the others. She looked at us, and we showed her respect. Truth be told, they were speaking in some bizarre language, the great language of idiots.

The best thing was that Angèle joined us at last. My mother put her foot in it, congratulating her right away for

79

her bravery in joining her husband in the danger zone... if she was planning to stay long... if she had a permit...

Angèle couldn't take her eyes off my military medal, staring at it intently.

I'd've loved to bang Angèle if I'd had some sleep first and the absolute security of a day or two ahead of me. But the medal didn't give me much sleep, although it did offer some measure of security. Except there was Cascade.

Next we were served a leg of lamb. We stopped thinking things over. I had three helpings, so did my father and Mr Harnache. His wife had two, Miss L'Espinasse one and a half. Seeing me eat so much, my mother smiled at me tenderly.

"Well, at least he hasn't lost his appetite," she said joyfully, for everyone to hear...

We never spoke about my ear. It was like the German atrocities, one of those unacceptable, unsolvable, dubious and frankly improper things that got in the way of their conception that everything in the world was redeemable. I was too ill and, above all, at that time, I lacked the education to establish in my madly buzzing head the ignominy of my old folks' behaviour and all their hopes, but I felt it weighing on me with each gesture, each time I wasn't doing so well, like an octopus, sticky as hell and heavy as a pile of shit. I felt their overwhelming, optimistic, hare-brained, nauseating stupidity, which they cobbled together to guard themselves against all evidence, turning a blind eye to the shame and the intense, extreme and bloody torture that was screaming at them below the very windows of the room where we were stuffing ourselves, as well as the humiliation of my own drama and decrepitude, which they refused to fully accept, since accepting it would be to despair, if only a little, of the world and of life, and they didn't want to despair of anything or anyone in spite of everything, including the war, which was marching past Mr Harnache's windows, battalion after battalion, with the thunder of its artillery rattling every pane of glass in the house. They were full of praise for my arm, though. That was a pleasing wound, allowing free rein to their optimism. The same for Cascade's foot, by the way. Angèle didn't say a thing, she wore hardly any make-up.

"Isn't she a lovely young thing, after all," my mother said after the salad [...].

They were all in cahoots. Not only were they celebrating my bravery, they were also lifting the morale of us wounded combatants.

We ate so much, the meal lasted a good two hours. When we were having dessert, the army chaplain, Canon Présure, dropped in to congratulate my parents. He spoke softly, like a lady. He drank his coffee as if it was liquid gold. He was sure of himself. My mother nodded with each word he spoke as he offered his congratulations. So did my father. They agreed with everything he said. It came from up on high.

"You see, my dear friend, Our Lord, in the midst of the most terrible tests to which he deigns to submit His creatures, still feels for each and every one of them an immense pity, an infinite compassion. Their suffering is His suffering, their tears are His tears, their anguish is His anguish..."

I assumed a moronic and contrite look and agreed with every word the chaplain said, like everyone else. I couldn't hear him very well because of the buzzing, which seemed to form an almost impenetrable helmet of noise around my head. His unctuous, venomous words reached me through those whistles, but only as if through a door with a thousand echoes.

My mother's mouth was slightly agape on account of the chaplain's elevated words. He was obviously used to it, and it didn't stop him from coming out with more pompous stuff, just as my mother didn't stop being devout, me buzzing and my father being an honest man. We drank some more cognac and *vieux* to toast my military medal again.

Cascade was taking swigs from Angèle's glass. He wouldn't let her finish hers, just to annoy her. He was gulping it down in front of her. He thought it was funny. It was like a kind of dance in Mr Harnache's dining room, a dance of emotions. It came and went in the middle of my buzzing. Nothing was stable any more. We were drunk, all of us. Mr Harnache had taken off his tie. We drank some more coffee. No one was listening to the chaplain any more. Except my mother, her head bobbing at the height of his mouth so as to follow his most elevated feelings concerning the perils of war and the supernatural charity of the Good Lord.

Angèle and Cascade were exchanging harsh words. I didn't understand all of it, but it was hard against hard.

"No, I ain't going…" she was saying. "I ain't going…"

She was taunting him. He'd told me, before we went, he'd like to shag her in the loo. Now she wouldn't go. Brilliant.

"I'll sing 'em a song, then!" he said.

And he got up off his chair. My father was very red in the face. The troops marched past, non-stop, clattering down the street like a heavy downpour of steel. The cavalry, then the artillery between the squadrons: trundling, rattling, swaying, echoing from one side to the other. You get used to it.

"He can't!" Angèle announced all of a sudden.

I saw it in her eyes. She was defiant. With her black pupils, her blood-red, provocative mouth, her harshly drawn eyebrows above her soft, attractive face. Better watch out. But Cascade was fully aware, no doubt about it.

"I'll sing a song whenever I feel like, and it ain't your ugly mug what's gonna shut me up!"

"Just you try," she said. "Just try and see what happens!"

I'll admit, she might well have been a little inebriated, but still there were things she couldn't just say and expect to get away with.

"What? What did you say, you slag!? How dare you defy your man in front of all these people? All you've done since I asked you to come here is turn tricks with them Tommies… Who do you think you belong to? Have you told them how I found you on the game in the Passage du Caire and how without me you'd never even've made enough dosh to show off your first blouse? One more word from you, you dirty slut, and I'll kick your stupid fucking face in! You deserve nothing less… piece of filth!…"

"Will you, now?" she said.

And more softly, concentrating hard on the words she'd surely rehearsed on her way over.

"You tell yourself that your Angèle must be as stupid as she was before… Well? Ain't that what you think? That she'll train you up another whore, ten more little whores, and three floozies to boot, plus all the other trash Monsieur drags off of the street, with their festering twats, and every month a brat in one belly or another that we then have to get rid of together, and each of 'em with two or three cases of the syph that cost an arm and a leg to treat, and that your Angèle'd stump up the cash, pay for the family's meds and booze with her cunt, her whole cunt and nothing but her cunt... No, my pumpkin, I've had enough, I don't give a shit about you. You're a dirty rotten son of a bitch, so rot away. Go and fuck yourself. It's each to his own now. That's it, ladies and gents, that was my evening edition!"

"Oh, Ferdinand, I'm biting my tongue! You heard what she said! I'll rip her guts out and serve 'em to you on a platter..."

Mr Harnache was just standing there. The chaplain, Miss L'Espinasse, everyone was in shock... He had already picked up the cake knife, though he wouldn't have done much harm with that.

My mother was listening to all those horrors. It was a horrible language she didn't understand. They held Cascade back. He sat down, his head swinging like a metronome. Luckily his wife was at the other side of the table. She didn't lower her eyes, though.

"Why don't you sing something for us, dear Cascade?" Mrs Harnache finally said, too dim to have understood a word. "I'll accompany you on the piano."

"All right!" he said, and he walked over to the piano, as if determined to murder someone.

He was staring down Angèle all the time. She'd calmed down a bit.

84

I know... tralala tralala that you're preeeetty...
Trala, trala
That your big, sweet eyes, errm... errm...
Have captured my heart!...
And that it's for liiife...
I know...

But then Angèle provoked him again. She got up very deliberately, in spite of the chaplain's attempt to hold her back.

"There's one thing you won't say, you disgusting piece of filth, and that's that you married twice... yeah, twice... and the second time with false papers. He ain't called Cascade, ladies and gents... not Cascade Gontran at all, and on top of that, he's a bigamist, yeah, a bigamist and married with false papers... and his first one, she's hawking her mutton in Toulon, that's right, and it's her what has his real name... his actual, proper name that is. Tell these ladies and gents if it's true or not..."

"Is that all you know? Tell me, is that all you know?" he kept on singing.

The assembled company didn't know what to do... Angèle got up to go and insult him in his face, up close like.

"And what if I did know something else?..."

"All right then, go ahead, tell 'em everything you know, while you're at it, the whole lot, you smart-arse. You'll see how this'll end for yer. You'll see how your Julien... how he'll crush you, you rotten egg, you jar of shit jam. Carry on, then, now that you've started. Just you carry on..."

"I don't need your permission, not in the slightest. I'll say it loud and clear who it was what bumped off a night guard at two in the morning on the fourth of August in the Parc des Princes... There's witnesses... Léon Crossepoil and that girl they call 'Dickbreaker', they'll confirm the story..."

"Great," he said. "Won't stop me singing, though. Listen, you dirty whore, whether I'll sing or not. Just listen. You'll get my head chopped off, do you hear me?... my head chopped clean off! But even with my head in a basket I'll keep singing if I feel like it, just to piss you off. Listen to this:

I know tralala trala that you're so pretty...
That your big, sweet eyes...
Have captured my heart...
And that it's for life...
I know...

"Do you want another verse? I'll sing them all to you [...]. All, so the shit will rise up and drown you. Listen to me, you lot. I can hit those highs, you can tell 'em that. Just know that for Cascade, a stupid little dipshit like you means fuck-all... I know all the verses, all of 'em, you hear? And I'll take you up the arse whenever it damn well pleases me."

"No siree, you will not take me up the arse! You will not take me up the arse! You, on your own, you have less balls than the worst faggot. You're a wimp, with your big mouth... you're not able to act like other men your age... You're a worse woman than me, you bitch. And don't contradict me. A worse woman than me."

"What!? What?..." Cascade blurted out, hesitant. "What's that you're saying?"

"What I'm saying is… that you shot yourself in the foot to be sent back to Paris to piss me off… Tell 'em it ain't true… Go on, tell them. That's the kind of guy he is!" she added, pointing at him as if he was a freak. It was quite a show.

Cascade was swaying on his rotting foot.

"I'll sing anyway. For France," he said in a tired voice. "And I'll tell you one more thing," he added. "You'll never shut me up, you hear me? The bird what will make me shut my cake hole ain't born yet… That's all I'm saying. Go and find yourself a man and see if he can shut me up. Is there anyone among you bunch of fuckers what can shut me up?"

No one replied, obviously. The chaplain quietly shuffled towards the door. The others didn't dare move. My mother was restraining herself from going over to him to calm him down with motherly, middle-class words.

And so he stood there, swaying and proud by the piano. His voice was rough, and he sang off-key. The funny thing was, he didn't try to make up with Angèle. Even though she was almost standing next to him. I noticed everything, cos it was like a nightmare. There's nothing you can do except let everything wash over you… He was a nightmare too. As was Angèle, really. In a way, it was good. She admitted as much.

"Yeah, as I was saying, it was you who shot yourself in the foot. That's what you wrote me… Don't say you didn't."

"So what if I did?" he asked.

"I sent your letter to the colonel. I did, too. Happy now? Are you gonna shut your filthy trap now? Well? Are yer?"

"No, I won't shut my trap, I'll never shut up, you disgusting piece of shit, you. I'd rather eat crap, d'you hear me? I'd rather they opened my gut with a sardine-tin key than to shut up cos you say so…"

"Let me accompany you on the piano, Mr Carcasse," Mrs Harnache interrupted.

She hadn't understood a single thing. She thought they were just having a tiff…

Angèle sat down next to my mother.

At that moment a cavalry regiment marched past.

I could hear the military band. I thought that Miss L'Espinasse had joined them and was playing the trumpet, blaring it out, despite wearing a helmet. A helmet that went up and up, like the notes. This wasn't normal.

"Cascade," I said. "Cascade, I… *Vive la France! Vive la France!*"

I collapsed. Everything in the dining room stopped, even Cascade's song. Everything was filled with my buzzing, the whole house, from top to bottom, and way beyond too, including the whole cavalry regiment, charging down the street and across the Place Majeure. And 120 mm mortars that were pounding the market. I was perfectly aware I was delirious. For an instant I saw my convoy again, my own little convoy, and wanted to follow it. Le Drellière was signalling something to me. Brave old Le Drellière… He did what he could… So did I… I ran and ran… and then I fell again.

So many years have passed that it's really hard to remember things exactly. What people said has almost become a lie. You should be wary. The past is a harlot. It dissolves into daydreaming and takes on little melodies on the way you never asked for. It comes wandering back to you, tarted up with tears and regrets. You can't take it seriously. When it gets like that, you turn to your dick for succour, immediately, so as not to lose the plot. It's the only way, the manly way. Get a tremendous boner but resist the temptation to beat your meat. Oh no. All the force will flow back up to your head, as they say. A bit Puritanical, but it does the trick. The past is fucked up. It gives itself up, for one instant, with all its colours, its lights and shades, even people's exact gestures – a memory taken by surprise. The past is a right pig, always drunk on forgetfulness, a sneaky bastard who's vomited all over your old affairs, that revolting junk you'd already put in order, stacked up that's to say, at the end of your wheezing days, lying in your very own coffin, waiting for death, that hypocrite. But after all, that's my problem, you'll say. So here's how things actually unfolded, or rather fell apart, after they brought me round and I was back at the hospital.

Before that, I even took my parents back to the station. They didn't know what to do with themselves. I insisted on tottering along with them. Cascade supported me, full of swagger on his crutches. The chaplain and L'Espinasse went their way. Angèle was nowhere to be seen. She slipped out through the kitchen. My father more than anyone else was troubled by what he'd heard and seen.

"Let's go, Clémence, let's go, quickly now," he coaxed my mother, who was limping almost as badly as Cascade, having sat down for so long. "Come quickly. After this train, there is only the eleven o'clock."

He was paler than the rest of us. He was the first who realized what had actually just happened. I was still buzzing too much, and Cascade still hadn't finished playing the fearless lad. Troops blocked our way every twenty metres. At last we got to the platform, in the nick of time, the whistle already blowing. Then it was just the two of us. It was high time we got back to the Virginal Secours.

"Shall we go back?" I asked Cascade, just in case.

"Of course," he said. "Where else should I go? To the ball?..."

I didn't say anything. Back on the ward it only took one look at the guys wrapped in their blankets and playing piquet to know that the rumour was already spreading. They never spoke much among themselves anyway, but this time they didn't try and ask us anything about what was going on in town like they normally did when we got back, the usual dirty talk about a bit of skirt, what we'd seen in the café, on the street, you know, typical questions from upstanding chaps. Nothing like that now.

It was Antoine, the little male nurse from the Midi, the one with a plaster cast next to the door, who filled me in when I walked past to have a slash.

"You know, two cops from the military police came by looking for Cascade, to ask him some questions, they said... You know anything about this?..."

I immediately walked over to Cascade to see what he had to say. Not much.

"It'll be all right," he said.

Night fell. The lights went out.

That's it, I told myself. The pigs are on to him. At dawn they'll come and nab him. I heard the clock strike nine, and then there was some artillery fire not far away, then some more, and then it was silent. Except for the usual trundling of trucks followed by the cavalry and that tremendous shuffling sound of countless footsloggers echoing up and along the walls whenever a battalion marched past. A whistle at the station. I needed to arrange all of that in my head before I could fall asleep, grab on tight to my pillow with both hands, stiffen my resolve, fight the anguish of never being able to sleep again, gather all my noises together, the racket inside my ear and outside, and then, little by little, I was able to snatch an hour or two, three of sleep, like trying to lift a colossal weight and then dropping it, failing catastrophically, again and again. You crack and can only think of dying, but you attack sleep once more, like hunting rabbits: one of 'em gets stuck in a ditch, gives up, gives in, but suddenly dashes off again, filled with hope. Sleep is a universe of unbelievable torture.

The next morning there was a lull. Some faraway explosions, that was all. The nurse brought the coffee round. I noticed she looked at Cascade differently. I was sure she knew something. It was a young girl from the convent. We never saw L'Espinasse any more. She was busy in the operating room, they told us. I secretly wondered what role she might have played in what was about to happen. After his cup of joe, Cascade went to the lavvy and returned to play piquet with Lard-Arse, as he was known, who had a heart condition and who was on the bed next to the bloke on the left. Lard-Arse wasn't actually fat, but his feet and belly were bloated on account of his albumin levels and a heart condition. That was all. It kept him in bed for three months. When he deflated all of a sudden, we didn't recognize him. Then something happened. Cascade won four games in a row. Cascade, who never won at anything. Camuset, a cripple who witnessed the whole thing, got excited and proposed a game of manilla with two wogs in the dressing room, while the nurses were having their lunch. That was forbidden. And again, Cascade kept on winning. He had a phenomenal streak of luck. A non-com from the Saint-Grévin ward next door walked by and couldn't believe his eyes. He took him to the other non-coms to play a game of poker with them. And still Cascade kept on winning. In the end he got up, all pale like, and quit playing.

"It ain't going well," he said.

"On the contrary," I said, "it's going swimmingly. It's going fabulously."

I just tried to boost his morale. He didn't agree. We went back under the covers for the inspection. Méconille came by with two floozies from outside and a bloke in civilian clothes we'd never seen before. When he stopped in front of Cascade's bed, my mate said:

"Major, sir," he said, "I'd like you to cut off my foot. I can't walk on it no more…"

Méconille looked embarrassed. Ordinarily he'd never refuse to lop off anything at all.

"We need to wait a little, my boy… It's too early…"

But it was obvious Méconille was holding something back. Normally he wouldn't have spoken like that. The other shitheads didn't think it was very natural of him neither. It was very fishy.

Cascade had tried. He sank back into his bed.

"Wanna go out?" he proposed.

We snuck into the kitchen, scored some rice, stuffed our faces and left.

I thought we were going to L'Hyperbole, but he didn't want to.

"Let's go to the countryside."

He managed to walk quickly, in spite of his foot. We still had to be careful not to be caught by the gendarmes. They were getting more of a pain in the arse by the day, compliance-wise. If we didn't have the proper permit, it turned into a drama each time, and L'Espinasse had to come and fetch us from the gendarmerie. English coppers were no better. The Belgians were even bigger arseholes. We advanced as if on a churned-up battlefield, from one landmark to the next, and at last we reached the countryside, as he called it, the fields behind the town, away from the front. Real peaceful like. You could hardly hear the artillery. We sat down on an embankment. We looked around. Far, far in the distance the sun was shining, and there were trees. It would be the height of summer soon. But the shadows cast by the passing clouds hovered over the fields of beetroot for long spells. I'll say it again, it was beautiful. The northern sun was weak. On the left there flowed a sleepy canal, lined by poplars, rustling in the wind. The canal zigzagged towards the hills to murmur its sweet nothings over there and continued until it dissolved into the blue of the sky, just before reaching the tallest of the three smokestacks on the horizon.

I'd've liked to say something, but held myself back. I wanted him to speak first after what happened the day before. That business with the cards also demanded an explanation. I don't think he cheated, though. It was just a fluke.

We saw some labourers and monks working in an enclosure, old guys all of them. They didn't have a care in the world and were pruning espaliers. It was the garden of their head monastery. Here and there in the ploughed fields, a peasant, holding up the sky with his backside in the air. Digging up beetroots.

"They're enormous around Peurdu-sur-la-Lys," I remarked.

"Come," said Cascade. "Let's see how far it goes."

"How far what goes?" I asked, surprised obviously.

It didn't seem a reasonable thing to do in our state, to go for a walk just for the hell of it.

"As long as it's not too far," I said.

We walked straight ahead, leaving the town behind us.

"We need to get a move on. We'll never get back on time."

He didn't respond. I told myself it wasn't worth being done for desertion now that I had my medal.

"One more kilometre," I said, "and then I'll turn back."

It's also true I vomited twice while we were walking.

"You never stop puking," he said.

It was mean of him to say that. Never mind. We never covered those thousand metres. We'd done less than three hundred when some clown stormed out of a sentry box with a bayonet fixed onto his rifle. He was fury personified.

After screaming at us for a bit, he asked where we were going.

"For a stroll in the countryside."

We kept out nerve. So he placed his rifle at his foot and explained that they were expecting an entire army to come along that road to reinforce the troops, and added that the Germans were just beyond those hills right now, at the end of the plain, right where the canal made a bend. In three or four hours tops, the shelling would start, and we'd get caught up in it if we stayed, so we had to get the hell out of there.

No sooner said than done. We hobbled on the double. There was no way out anywhere. After what we'd heard, we went back to the canal. Turns out Cascade had made us walk in some absurd circle with his stupid whims. We sat back down on the embankment of the canal. I saw a deep frown appear on my mate's forehead, after which he started to walk towards the water.

"You make me laugh," I said to cheer him up and drag him out of that cesspool he'd been wallowing in since that notorious lunch at the Harnaches the night before.

"You make me laugh. You can't be sure of nothing. You don't even know for sure if Angèle actually did any of that shit she said, and yet you're in a blue funk... She's a show-off, and I'm sure she said all that nonsense in front of the others just to humiliate you... and that she has your letter in her pocket..."

Cascade snarled when he heard what I said, on purpose, to show his contempt.

"It's clear you ain't well... you don't see how it all fits together..."

I didn't understand. So I kept my trap shut. Didn't stop me from having an opinion, though. I still had some money, twenty-five francs from my parents, and he must have had at least as much from Angèle.

"I'll go and find us some plonk," I proposed.

"Get yourself three litres. It'll do you good."

Those were his words.

There was a little bistro at the mouth of the canal, near the town. It took me just under a quarter of an hour to get there and back.

"You're not joining me?" I asked.

"Don't feel like it," he replied. "I'll go and see if I can't find a fishing line at the lock to go fishing."

I went on my way, quietly, absorbed in my thoughts. Then I heard a big *splash!* in the water behind me. Before I could even turn round, I'd understood. I walked back. There, at the lock, there was a big splashing bundle. Cascade, of course. We were the only ones at the canal.

"Are you drowning?" I shouted.

I don't know why. It was instinct. His head was sticking out of the water. His arms too. He wasn't drowning at all. He tried to clamber out of the mud. I went over to him and laughed in his face.

"Not deep enough, is it?" I told him. "You fuckwit. It's not deep enough. You're in the shit and that's it."

Cascade looked dreadful. Luckily there was no one else to see us. It was enough of a pain in the arse as it was.

"You can't drown yourself in there, you twerp. There's no depth. I could've told you…"

With some difficulty on account of his foot, he dragged himself back onto the bank and lay down in the grass.

"You may not have drowned, but you'll catch a cold and get the shivers," I told him.

He didn't protest.

"Go and find us some rum and leave me the fuck alone."

That's how he replied to me. I went back again. This time I brought back a whole litre of rum, a litre of beer, two litres of white wine and three huge brioches, bigger than a man's head. We leant back against a poplar and pigged out good. We felt a whole lot better with our bellies full. He was drying up.

"I want to go fishing."

"I don't know how to," I said.

"I'll show you."

OK, then. Suddenly I felt very pissed. I walked back along the embankment to the bistro to rent some fishing lines. They gave me some, along with a little tin full of maggots. We had some more booze and decided to give it a go. We chucked the corks in the water.

No sooner had his touched the water than he caught an actual pike, and then lots of little fish, enough to fill a shopping bag. I didn't catch anything, naturally. He had all the luck in the world. Come five o'clock, the bottles were empty. At six, it was getting dark.

"We need to bring back the fish," he said.

We got under way. We returned to the Virginal Secours without any hiccups.

"It's like the miraculous catch of fish," said the sister cook, who was also the hospital's messenger.

We paid no attention to what she said. Still, in those conditions you don't stay drunk. After vomiting two or three times, I was completely sober again. We were too preoccupied, on high alert, you might even say. We had the night ahead of us. And it promised to be a dark and treacherous one. First we had some grub, as usual. But afterwards, Cascade refused to go to bed. He paced up and down, from the loo to the windows in the corridor. L'Espinasse did her rounds, and when the concierge dimmed the gaslights, she slipped behind his back without seeming to notice him, and then she halted and stood still in front of me.

"Is it you?" I asked. "Is it really you?"

She didn't answer. She stayed there for another minute or so, and then she seemed to glide away in the semi-darkness.

Then the night began in earnest.

Cascade was sitting on his bed instead of lying down. He started to read, him, who normally never read a single word. He read by the light of a candle. His neighbour was not best pleased, neither was the bloke opposite, all the more since there was two bods who couldn't stop moaning and another who needed a piss all the time. The night nurse came and blew his candle out. He lit it again. It was gone eleven already. He'd read all the newspapers. He looked for more stuff to read on the table in the middle. He lit another candle. Then the Moroccan artilleryman with cystitis, the one near the entrance, the one who snored louder than all the rest and a real thug, he flung his crutch across the room. It flew within a hair's breadth of the candle. Cascade got up to sock it to him. They nearly came to blows. They were screaming abuse at each other.

"Right," said Cascade, "if it's like this, I'll go and read on the crapper. And I won't have to look at your ugly mugs neither, seeing as I'm stopping you from having a nice old wank, you bunch of fucking pansies."

Those were his words. Then this old git from the railway troops at the other end of the ward, a real RAT* and a proper diabetic, he got up and hurled his pot across the row of twenty-two beds, spraying everyone with piss. The pisspot smashed into a window. Two sisters came up, and we all went quiet. Then it kicked off again. In the end Cascade cleared off.

"I don't want to go to sleep no more," he said. "Fuck the lot of youse."

He wanted to light his candle once again.

"Go and fuck yourself, you dirty bastard. I hope they actually shoot this guy, so he'll stop breaking our balls."

They were really sick of him.

So Cascade went back to the bog, because that was the only place the light was on all night.

It must have been one in the morning.

"Hey, Ferdinand, have you got something to read?"

I looked in the nurses' room. I knew they kept their books in a hat box. Copies of *Les Belles Images*,* they were, whole stacks of them. Cascade took 'em all. He'd developed a passion, it has to be said.

"Close the door," I said to him, "in case someone comes…"

He shut the door. One hour passed, then another. He was still inside. I didn't dare get up, in case the others would start shouting again.

At last, the first light of the day appeared over the roof opposite… the one laced with strips of zinc.

Then a voice that made everyone sit up, even though it was a quiet voice, an odd voice for a gendarme, a woman's voice almost, but very precise, a voice that knew what it wanted, and it came from the entrance of the Saint-Gonzef ward:

"You have among you a certain private Gontran Cascade of the 392nd infantry regiment, have you not?"

"He's in the loo next to you, sir," the artilleryman next to the entrance bellowed.

The door opened.

Out came Cascade. *Click*, *click*, sounded the handcuffs.

Another copper was waiting for him at the end of the corridor. We didn't really have time to see Cascade, his face I mean. It was still too dark.

Four days later he was shot in Péronne, where his regiment, the 418th infantry, was stationed and enjoyed fourteen days of rest.

They annoyed the hell out of me, those other bods on the ward, with their tales of heroism. As soon as we found out Cascade had ended up in front of a firing squad, they all started to talk rubbish about their bravery. They were all heroes all of a sudden. You'd think they were making up for being such dicks with him in his last hours. They were soiling him. They didn't mention him by name, but it was obvious to me that the whole business bothered them. Hearing them talk, you'd think they hadn't been scared for one second during the war. The old railway trooper Giboune, who shat his pants whenever an aeroplane flew over our ward at midday, he wouldn't stop crowing about a tiny scratch he had. It had taken at least three machine guns to give him his flesh wound in the buttocks. Things like that. Abloucoum, a Moroccan soldier with boils, who could only think about his fistula, he'd never seen a bullet up close in his life. This didn't stop him from telling us how he'd taken a whole camp of indigenous fighters back in Morocco, all by himself, just by waving a torch and a special kind of cry. Scared them stiff, he claimed. It was on account of Cascade they all started to spout bullshit. Secretly, I think the whole affair had upset many of 'em terribly. With these tall tales they tried to ward off strokes of fate. I was better shielded than them because of my medal and my fabulous citation, but I still didn't trust anything or anyone. The whole experience made me age a month with every week that passed. In a war that's the speed you have to go at if you don't want to end up in front of a firing squad. Take it from me.

At any rate, they were all jealous. Even if I never showed them my medal. I only pinned it on when I went into town. With Cascade gone, I had no one to lean on should I teeter during one of my dizzy spells. I didn't really fraternize with the other piss-pants. Everyone on the ward was turning into a parasite. Heroes or not, we were just a bunch of hypocrites. The proof is we never talked about L'Espinasse, nor what happened downstairs in the morgue. We only talked about trifles. The most seriously wounded, the biggest drivellers, they never showed their true intentions. The dying weren't sincere neither. I'd seen some of them pretend to die for a lark when L'Espinasse walked by. It's a fact. I studied that bitch with her heavenly veils, fondling those who were the furthest gone, treating herself to gratifying catheter sessions, and I told myself that perhaps, at the end of the day, she might have a point. She was looking for sincerity, which the others didn't have. People like L'Espinasse gave me courage. When she came by that evening for a kiss, I stuck my tongue deep into her mouth, licking her gums. I hurt her a little. I knew it was sensitive. I was beginning to understand her, I'll be honest. Which meant she was getting attached to me. One day she said to me in a hushed tone:

"Ferdinand, I've come to an agreement with the military authorities of the garrison. Because of the trouble your ear is giving you, you will be allowed to sleep in the little pavilion in the back of the garden until your appearance before the military board. We've put a bed in there, and you'll get more rest than on the ward. No one will disturb you…"

You should've heard her. I was beginning to understand that sly cow. What a strange ploy, isolating me in her pavilion like that. Anyway, I decamped and freed up my bed for someone else.

"You won't see me again, you arsewipes. You'll all be sent back to the trenches, and I'll be stuffing my face with you lot once you've turned into vegetables down there, in between them beetroots and the latrines."

They had a right laugh. They could take a joke, that's for sure.

"Shitface! Better look after your filthy innards, you dirty bastard. You'll trip over that medal of yours."

They shot right back.

I moved in. I walked around the pavilion. It was all right. It looked like an honest kind of place, right at the back of the garden. Real isolated. What can I say? They brought me my grub. She said I could go out between ten and five.

I took the little streets. I vomited discreetly in some porch or other whenever I felt sick. Apparently, there was fighting on all sides now, forty kilometres away, in front of us and behind. I wondered where to go if I had to scarper. Everywhere you go, the earth is putrid, I told myself. You should be able to get to a country where they don't kill each other. But I didn't have my health, no money, no nothing.

It's revolting when for months you've seen nothing but convoys of men in all kinds of uniforms parading in the streets like strings of sausages, men in khaki, reservists, men in horizon blue and apple green, nothing but meat carried on wheels to be minced by that great meat grinder of fools. They march straight ahead, hum a tune, have a quaff, come back horizontal, bleed, have another quaff, sob, yell, they're rotting away already, then a rain shower, the wheat grows, other idiots arrive by ship, it blows its horn, in a hurry to get everyone off board, the ship turns round huffing and puffing, it shows its backside, that beautiful ship on the pier, and then it's off again, cleaving the frothy waves, looking for more… Always happy, those stupid bastards, always partying. The more of them are ground up, the more beautiful the flowers bloom the next spring. That's what I say. Hurray for shit and good wine! It's all for free!

What did I risk if I dropped in at L'Hyperbole? Nothing. I'd give that little Destinée the news, if she didn't know already. But Angèle had already filled her in. Angèle wasn't about to leave town. Of course not. It was simple, she knew her way around here. I got that. The Place Majeure was getting busier all the time, the crossroads of the world. It was one on top of the other. They'd put up footbridges to make it easier to cross the intersecting streets. People were dying every day with all the shelling and the high concentration of squaddies, but in the area they were doing a roaring trade. On the market it was bedlam. People were snatching flowers from each other's hands. It's amazing how well wreaths sell in time of war. And for lots of reasons. There was an air-raid siren. In case of an attack from the air, people were supposed to go and hide in shelters. It was a sight to behold. Once I saw a whole battalion sitting it out in L'Hyperbole for the whole hour the alarm sounded. By the time they left, they'd smashed up the entire place, not a single glass was left in one piece. They'd even drunk the crystalware. I'm not making it up. A 75 mm gun got so scared, it went up to the notary's office on the first floor, horses and all. Honest to God. Just to say that things went berserk.

When things calmed down, Angèle, a widow now, would venture into the street. To begin with, I was afraid to speak to her. Like before, she was standing near the English HQ, diagonally opposite L'Hyperbole, where I observed her from behind a half-curtain. Initially Destinée hadn't really clocked what fate had befallen Cascade. She was not the sharpest tool in the box. She'd cry hot tears when she thought of him, but without really understanding why. She still shared the same room above the café with Angèle, since that's how it'd been arranged. Plus Destinée was knackered from serving drinks by the barrel to all the punters at the thirty-five tables of L'Hyperbole, all by herself, until ten at night, having started at a quarter past six in the morning, which is when the place was allowed to open. Angèle was unbelievably wicked, as I found out later, and she managed to eat Destinée's pussy when they went up to their room, making her come two, three times. The more tired Destinée was from waiting on tables, the more Angèle got excited and wanted her to climax. And the harder she had to work at it, the better she liked it. People are bonkers.

In a word, it felt a bit immoral to go look for Angèle after what had happened, but she showed no surprise at my return. We went to another café to talk. I didn't dare reproach her. Instead, she turned me on. I'd have liked an explanation, though. But she avoided that part of the conversation. I dropped the subject of Cascade and moved closer to her in order to feel her up a bit. She let me. It wasn't easy, on account of my arm, which nearly made me scream when I squeezed too hard, and my ear, which filled itself with noise to the point of exploding when my face got flushed. But I got hard, which was the main thing. Behind my bleeding lumps of meat, I imagined her arse sticking out in hopeful expectation. I saw life return. Good old Angèle. She felt I was aroused. Her eyes were dark and velvety, full of sweetness, like in Cascade's song, the one he'd never sing again. She stole my heart. She paid for all the drinks. I didn't want to ask my parents for no more money. I was proud and disgusted.

"You're right," she said encouragingly.

I watched her leave and cross the Place Majeure. She walked between the battalions on leave like the very essence of joy and happiness. Her buttocks ploughed a graceful furrow through one hundred tons of smelly, tired, sprawling flesh of twenty thousand men, all dying of thirst. The square smelt so bad that for a moment she quickened her step. And then she went back and powdered her face, her favourite gesture, at a short distance from the headquarters of general V.W. Purcell. At around eleven, general V.W. Purcell would leave in his yellow-and-purple cabriolet drawn by two chestnut horses to go for a little tour of the trenches. He'd drive himself without making a fuss. He was a man of the world. Two mounted officers followed him at a considerable distance, B.K.K. Olisticle, an Irish major, and Lieutenant Percy O'Hairie, a real girl, what with his fine traits and slender hips.

Angèle's game was to hit on English officers, nothing but upper-class Brits, the type that's afraid to be seen shagging. I was on to her after one, two days. I didn't dare ask her to go up to her room together. It was delicate. But then she came with a proposal.

"Hey, listen," she said. "You with your medal and all, you're nice, you look good. You know what I was thinking last night in bed with Destinée... No?... Well, I told myself, you'd be perfect for this, you know, creating a scandal... You could pretend to be my husband... I used to play this trick in Paris with Dédé 'Small Hands'. It works a treat, and it's good."

I allowed her to explain.

"So, I get undressed, you know, as usual, I let the guy rub up against me a bit... When he's hard, real hard, I'll suck his cock... Then you enter into the room without knocking. I'll just pretend to turn the key. I'll shout, Shit! It's my husband... You should see the look on their English faces when this happens... Once I picked up this guy in the Olympia, and he passed out... And it's them what offer to pay you, always. You don't have to do nothing. They know... Me and Dédé pulled this one twenty times or more, it's a piece of cake, I'm telling you... You can't get any more stupid than an Englishman with a hard-on... They all turn into idiots the moment they see you come in. They don't know how to excuse themselves for having their dicks out. It's hilarious. Meanwhile, I pretend you've caught me in the act. I start screaming, but secretly I roll around laughing. It's like a scene from the pictures. You'll see. Are you in?… You won't regret it, but I'll decide what your cut is…"

"Deal!" I said.

I was in favour of emancipation at home too. I was fed up of being skint and in pieces, my head, my mind, from my ear down to my arsehole. I wanted to put myself together again one way or another.

"I'll look after you. I'll make you fuck like you've never fucked before… And if you're nice, if you're a good boy, I'll let you lick my bunghole the way I like it… It'll be like we was married. First off, though, I'm two years older than you, so I'm the one in charge…"*

She sure knew how to tickle my fancy with what she said. My imagination went hopping mad for joy listening to her speak. I couldn't stand it any longer. As long as there's vice, there's pleasure. Still, I thought about Cascade for a sec, but then I turned round and the thought was gone. The present was all about Angèle, all about sex. That way my salvation lay. Plus, it was hardly the moment to get eaten up by scruples. This time round, I wouldn't be held back by such things as good manners. The blow that had shaken me to the core had relieved me of the enormous burden of having a conscience, of decency, as they say. That, at least, I'd gained. Ha! On closer inspection, I no longer had any. I'd had enough of dragging myself from one day to the next, my skull a wasteland, and, above all, of suffering night after night, my head a factory floor, feeling like I was being parachuted. I didn't owe humanity anything, at least not the humanity you imagine when you're twenty and suffer from scruples the size of cockroaches, scuttling all over your mind and everything else. Angèle would do nicely as a replacement for my father, and for Cascade, who in a way belonged to the time before the war, truth be told. Angèle knew how to enjoy herself, she had a taste for all things foreign and was fond of exchanges.

Great. If I had to replace Cascade, I ought to show I was up to it from the get-go, that's to say, I had to be much more streetwise. I weighed things up, and then I took the plunge.

"All right," I told her. "I'm in."

She took me to her room, I mean Destinée's room, to show me what to do. A kind of general rehearsal, so to speak. I had to knock on the door, which was to the left of the middle bed between the washbasin and the trunk. The room was actually a kind of junk room and stank of sweat. It was a dump, for sure, but that made the whole thing more exciting, she explained.

"'Cos, you see, these guys have enough luxury where they come from..."

To show me she'd stick to her side of the deal, she took her clothes off. It was the first time I'd seen her in her undies. Naked she was shapely and not very tall, rather petite in fact, delicate but sturdy. I could immediately see what her main attraction was. Leaving to one side her eyes, it was that skin of hers... The light on the skin of redheads is terrible for horny bastards. It's a mirage like no other, nothing like it. You learn to put up defences against different kinds of floozies. If it comes to it, you have your own special way to resist the wavey skin of blondes, or velvety brunettes, that's to say, the most luscious ones, the best turned out.

It's tempting to touch their flesh, like touching life itself, spreading your fingers all over. It's firm, but it also gives way a little. It's the fruit of paradise, no doubt about it. Its attraction has no limits, but still, you can resist it if you must... But redheads... they immediately stir the animal in you. It comes out, asks no questions, recognizes its sister and is content.

There I was, going down on Angèle, right on top of the straw mattress. It made my head buzz and throb something awful. I thought it'd be the end of me. She came though, two, three times, unstoppable. It was child's play to her. I bit the inside of her thighs. Just to punish her a little. Now she was really beginning to enjoy herself. All the same, I was knackered. I got up to vomit a little. I pretended it was just spit.

I still had to rehearse the closet act, though. It was getting late. We looked at the Place Majeure in the distance again, teeming with life as always, all that flesh milling about in between air-raid sirens. The lights were on at the English headquarters, even though that was forbidden.

"Don't forget to be here at one tomorrow. Wait in the room until I bring one back. We mustn't be seen together in the street. As soon as you hear footsteps on the stairs, hide yourself and watch through the hole. When I'm naked and he's in position, you knock and enter like you own the place and act all astonished... The rest will be a doddle, you'll see."

I hurried back to my pavilion. It worried me, being isolated in the back of the garden. I couldn't make any plans. There was still so much to be afraid of. L'Espinasse came to change my dressing and put some drops in my ear. When she left, there was a noise of wind and torrential rain and howling dogs. You can just imagine what it was like.

I grabbed on tight to my pillow and tried to get some kip. I always had to make a huge effort not to give in to the anguish of never being able to sleep any more on account of the buzzing that just wouldn't stop, ever, until my dying day. I'm sorry I keep saying it, but that's how it is. Never mind, let's not get sad over this. As I was saying, the next morning I was there, inside the closet, I mean, between the trunk and the washbasin. I didn't have to wait long, an hour maybe, and then I heard a soft voice with a nice timbre, as they say. I had a peek. It was a Scotsman. He took off his little skirt and got starkers in a jiffy. He was a ginger too, and as muscular as a horse. He started slowly, not saying a word. It looked like she was being mounted by a chestnut horse. It was straightforward. First he walked, then trotted, then galloped, and then he jumped over a hurdle, sinking his dick into her, and again, without any violence. He was banging her beautifully. He penetrated her so deeply she grimaced. I did say she was fragile. She looked in my direction. Come on, come on, she mouthed.

She grimaced even harder. She couldn't help but climax. So did he. He squeezed her buttocks so hard it seemed like she was splayed all over his belly, that's how hard he squashed her.

It was fascinating to watch his hands at work. They were like clamps on Angèle's skin, spread wide, muscular and as hairy as the rest of him. I should've come out of the closet at that moment and play the furious hubby. This was my chance. Especially after he'd come and was taking a rest, still not saying a dicky bird and with his penis exposed. He just sat there breathing hard, as if he'd been running too fast. I wondered how he would've reacted.

As soon as he caught his breath, he mounted her again. She was still panting. He started the whole business all over. She hardly reacted. He was very powerful, this Scotsman. Even in the depths of my poky closet I could still hear the field guns in the distance, from both sides of the town now. I had a hard-on. My head was buzzing. I nearly suffocated too, there in my closet, especially since I had to stoop to see them. I was wondering if he wasn't going to do her in the way he was pumping away between her thighs, the stud. But no. In the end she let herself be carried along like a parcel. Her body was more than supple. She just moaned a little. He lay down on his back and put her on top of him. The blood had drained from her face. I was so caught up in this spectacle, I stuck my face to the door. Suddenly it flew open and I surprised them in the middle of their frenzy. This is going to end badly, I told myself. A big fella like that is surely going to floor me... Not at all. Not so much as a quiver. He continued to plough Angèle. Even more vigorously, perhaps, now that I was watching him. It threw me, I'll admit. Angèle was barely conscious on top of this guy, who was stark bollock naked and hairy as hell. She didn't react to anything. She allowed herself to be bounced about, groaning softly. Now there was a guy who had not fucked in months. *Giddyap!* He broke into a galop again. She tried to get off of him and yell.

But he stifled her scream with his mouth. In the end he had another massive, brutal climax, clenching his arse-cheeks as if they'd shoved something big up his arsehole.

I really thought it'd be the end of her the way he ejaculated. He contracted his buttocks so hard on top of Angèle that deep dimples appeared on both sides. And then he relaxed, as if he too was dead, and he stayed there, lying on top of her, spent, for at least three minutes. I didn't budge. He let out a grunt and looked in my direction. He gave me a friendly smile. Not in the least angry. He put one foot on the floor, got up and got dressed next to the window, still not saying a word to me. He fumbled in his pocket, took out a pound and put it in Angèle's hand. She was still lying on her back, out for the count, trying to get back to her senses.

She came out of her stupor when she felt the pound in her hand. She looked at both of us. She was gobsmacked. The Scotsman had put his clothes back on, including his little skirt, sword belt and swagger stick. He was as pleased as Punch. He bent down to kiss her, gave her a peck on the cheek and left, still without uttering a word, quietly shutting the door. Not a worry in the world, this guy. Angèle was finding it hard to sit up. She stroked her lower belly with both hands. She gingerly moved to the washbasin to wash out her vulva. She was still panting. So was I.

"It was like a storm," I said, always the poet.

"Maybe," she replied, "but the prize idiot is you."

I had no comeback.

"Tomorrow," she said, "you won't wait in the closet. You'll place yourself on the corner opposite, on the terrace of L'Hyperbole and keep a close eye on the window. Got it?

And when you see me draw the curtain, you come up... you don't knock, you just barge in. Understood?"

"Yes," I said.

"Now fuck off."

I wanted to kiss her.

"Here, have some of his jizz."

She held out her palm, covered in spunk... I didn't insist. I didn't want to upset her. Couldn't afford to.

I didn't have such a great night neither. I was wondering how Angèle would react if I messed up again with the scam involving her punters. She was my only hope, Angèle was.

In Peurdu-sur-la-Lys they were going to evacuate all the sick and wounded, especially those able to walk. The town was no longer safe. Far from it. The Place Majeure was one dizzying chaos, on account of the explosions. The cattle troughs had been destroyed. Because the town was in the enemy's sights, the regiments passing through were always scrambling for places to hide, running through the little streets as if a fire had broken out. There were moments of panic worse than during the fighting, but much partying too, given that the cafés remained open until the last minute. In L'Hyperbole I once saw a bloke come in, a Zouave. He was pushed all the way to the bar by a crowd of pongos taking cover from an incoming Minnie at the arcades. He had just enough time to order a white wine with syrup. Then he bent double. Dead as a doornail. We all sat in a daze at our tables. You had to drink fast. Enough said.

The next day at one, ahead of time, I placed myself where Angèle had told me to. I waited to see how things would pan out. As it happened, it was almost calm. The never-ending baggage train, the thirst and dust of convoys that kept on coming, the swaying of the little trucks taking whole armies into the depths of war, one wheel just about as wobbly as the other, the rattle of falling chains, two nags continuously bumping into each other, two thousand three hundred axles screeching for grease, the echoes that sounded like a hailstorm and that filled the streets until everything had passed – that whole racket had died down. All you could hear was the whinny of a horse [...]. An hour went by. Angèle still has to make her first catch of the day, I thought. Siesta time was over, which is when the English most like to fuck, being too drunk in the evening. Nevertheless, there was people coming out of the English HQ, well-fed types. And fat and old and young, the whole lot: on horseback, on foot, even by car. What if she'd simply sacked me? I wondered.

I watched things for another hour. Destinée came up to me. She didn't have a clue what was going on. I didn't explain. She was giving me the eye. Sure.

Right. The curtain moved, I was certain of it, on the second floor. I ran like the clappers. I was determined as hell. I even overcame my dizziness. One floor. Two floors. No knocking. I burst into the room. The guy on the bed on top of Angèle jumped up. It was an old coot wearing nothing but khaki pants. He'd taken off the rest. His face showed great terror. Mine too. We were scared, the both of us. Suddenly Angèle had a laughing fit.

"It's my husband!" she said, cracking up. "It's my husband!"

He quickly put his willy back in his pants. He was shaking all over, as was I. He was too afraid to notice we were having him on. His fear gave me courage.

"*Money! Money!*" I told him. "*Money!*"* I said, trembling but buoyed up [...].

Angèle joined in:

"*Mon mari!* Yes! *Mon mari! My husband! My husband!*"*

She was sitting on the bed, legs akimbo, gesticulating wildly. She stressed the *band* in "husband", a word she'd just picked up.

"This old geezer's as meek as a lamb. Give him a smack in the face, Ferdinand," she encouraged me in plain French.

It's true this guy was perfect for a beginner like me. Days come and go, and none of 'em are alike. I pulled my arm back and gave him a left hook, not too hard. I hit him on the middle of his cheek. Deep down, I was afraid of hurting him.

"Hit him proper, you stupid bastard," she said.

I tried again. It was easy. He didn't put up a fight. He had grey hair and must have been at least fifty. So I landed one squarely on his schnozz. He started to bleed. Then Angèle changed her tune. She started to cry and threw herself around his neck.

"Protect me, protect me," she whispered to him. "Take me now. Fuck me now," she told me quietly. "Fuck me, you blockhead."

I hesitated.

"Just do as I say, you big poof. Get your dick out."

So I got my dick out. But she's still hanging on the old geezer's neck. She embraced him, and I embraced her. She twisted her body so I could easily stick it in. She was crying all over his face. When she came, she gushed like a geyser. The bloke turned every colour from sheer emotion, it has to be said. He was holding his nose. She was fiddling with his fly. We were all panting.

"Now hit me," she commanded.

This time I didn't hold back. I gave her a dozen smacks hard enough to fell a donkey. The old coot thought the bloodbath was starting all over.

"No! No!" he said.

He jumped towards his uniform jacket on the chair, took out a wad of banknotes and showed me the dough.

"Don't take it," she told me. "Get dressed and scram."

I did my buttons up and tucked my shirt in. The old codger, though, insisted. He really wanted me to take the dosh. I didn't understand what he was saying. My head was buzzing too much. I went to the bucket they used as a toilet to puke. He took pity on me and helped me by holding my head. No grudge at all.

Angèle explained to him in English:

"*My husband, his* honour made him sick! Malade! Sick!…*"

In the middle of my puking I started to laugh. The old punter was very hairy. His chest and shoulders were all covered in grey hair. Naturally, he didn't know where to look.

"I'm sorry! I'm sorry!" he said.

I left without accepting his apologies, with dignity, you know. I waited for half an hour on the stairs. And then I went back to my room. I couldn't wait any longer. I couldn't stand up straight. As long as it's worked, I told myself.

After mess, Angèle herself came to see me with a smile on her face. That put me at ease.

"How much did he give you?" I asked.

"None of your business," she said, "but it all went well."

Still, I noticed she was pale.

"First off, he's not what you think he is, the Englishman. He's better than that."

"Oh?" I said. "And how did you find that out?"

"We had a chat, that's all."

She hinted that I wouldn't understand the finer details.

"So? What did you decide?"

"All right. Here's the story. When you left, I told him that you was an awful brute. That you tortured me! That you was jealous and depraved like no other!... The more I told him, the more he wanted to know... Then I wanted to see if he was really rich. You never know with these people. They always lie when it comes to dough... But I wanted to be sure before committing to this plonker, cos guess what he proposed? To take me straight to England..."

"Did he actually?"

"And there he wants to set me up. How old you think he is?..."

"About fifty?"

"Fifty-two. He showed me his papers, the lot. I made him show me everything. He's an *engineer*...* of the Corps of Royal Engineers... In real life he's an engineer too, no, more than that, he has three factories in London. That's how it is."

I could see Angèle was well happy, but I could also see her bugger off for good.

"What about me?"

"He's not mad at you, my lollipop. I made him see that deep down you're a good guy, except for your serious flaws and violent streak, which you got from the war, and that he had to forgive you, cos you received a massive blow to your ear and noodle, and that you even was the most courageous fella in your regiment, seeing as they'd given you a medal. He wants to see you again... He wants to do something for you too..."

"Fuck me!"

I couldn't believe it.

"Tomorrow, at three, we'll all meet at the bistro at the mouth of the canal, you know, near the lock. Now go on, have yourself a nice little wank. Toodle-oo. I don't want to make Destinée wait. She's afraid of the dark and shuts the door downstairs."

And off she was.

Fifteen hours on the clock before the meeting, I told myself. I preferred not to leave my room. I felt fate all around me, so fragile it was like the creaking of the floorboards and the furniture as I paced up and down the room. In the end I stopped moving. I just waited. Towards midnight I heard the swoosh of fabric in the corridor. It was L'Espinasse.

"Are you all right, Ferdinand?" she asked from behind the door.

Should I answer her, I asked myself. Should I answer? Then softly, as if almost asleep, I replied:

"I'm all right, Madame, I'm all right..."

"Well, goodnight, then, Ferdinand, goodnight."

She didn't come in.

The next day, at the canal, I went to the terrace of the little bistro. I walked past the lock and waited behind a poplar, fifty meters or so away, invisible. I kept a lookout. I didn't want anyone to spot me. First watch. I waited. I was beginning to understand how to make use of nature. It was a waiting game. She was the first to arrive and sit down. She ordered a shandy. Funny, those fashions from 1914 didn't last long. Tastes were the exact opposite in 1915. She wore a felt cloche hat that looked like a helmet. She wore it low with a little veil, which made her eyes even bigger. Now her face was all eyes. They unnerved me even from that great distance. There's no doubt Angèle pulled at the mysterious strings of my soul, as they say.

The other dickhead, the English *ingenir*, arrived quietly along the towpath. He had a little pot belly, truth be told. The curious thing was, he looked more like a fifty-year-old with his clothes on than in the nude.

His wore a khaki uniform, like the rest of the engineers, and he had to be with HQ, cos he sported a red band on his cap, and of course a swagger stick and boots that must have cost him at least five hundred francs.

He sat himself down in front of Angèle's eyes, and they started to chew the fat. When their chat was well underway, I approached with a limp, to look more like an invalid. I gave him a cold look, but he seemed decent, good-natured even. I sat down. I relaxed. He looked at me with tenderness, I've got to say. So did Angèle. It made me feel a bit like I was their child. We ordered four small bottles of beer and a full meal for me. The two of them were spoiling me. When I think that just opposite Cascade had tried to drown himself... I dragged that memory out of the mud. And pushed it back down again. I didn't say anything. Angèle sure has the memory of a goldfish. The major asked for my name. I gave it him. He gave me his. Cecil B. Purcell he was called. Major Cecil B.

Purcell KBE.* He handed me his calling card. It said it right there. He was with the Royal Corps of Ingeneers.* It said so on another bit of paper. His wallet was bulging, stuffed with banknotes in fact. I eyeballed them. With what was there, you could travel around the world twelve times over, and again and again, until you were nowhere to be found.

"Listen, Ferdinand, Uncle Cecil wants to take the two of us to England."

That's what she'd been calling him since the day before, Uncle Cecil. Looking at me closely, his eyes became moist. He loved me, like. She noticed his loving look. We got lucky, no doubt about it.

The beautiful sun of great occasions shone on both sides of the canal. Summer was celebrating with us, welcoming us with its warmth.

Another bottle of beer. Everyone and everything was wishing me well. The three of us were mumbling, caressing each other's shoulders affectionately in the warmth. A beautiful friendship. Stuttering and stammering have become second nature to me, so I came across as quite pissed. All I have to do is let my circus and little personal memories take over and that's it. With my torrent of music on the tap, I'm transported to a surreal world in a jiffy.

Purcell KBE stroked my hair. He was having a good time too. All was going well. Angèle hadn't forgotten why we were there, though.

"Sort yourself out, Ferdinand," she whispered to me as we were getting up. "We'll skedaddle in two days. Tell that hag of yours you want to convalesce in London, that he's family, that he'll look after you."

That's what we settled on.

It's true, I had all the requisites. England hardly held good memories for me, though. But it was miles better than what they made me suffer afterwards.

"All righty," I said.

I felt happy too. I was the one leading the two of them. We walked towards the towpath, arm in arm, leaning on each other. We didn't go very far. Purcell walked in the middle. We sat down on the grassy embankment. From here, we had a good view of the lock where Cascade... Anyway... His song welled up to my lips:

> I know...
> That you're so pretty...
> That your big, sweet eyes...

Purcell liked to hear me sing. He liked everything about me. It broke my heart. I couldn't manage more than two verses. Purcell wanted to know the whole song and told us to write to him.

Those fucking field guns never stopped. And when they did, I'd reproduce the noise by myself. Even today I can still fire a perfect round of artillery in my head. All the same, the evening came to a close.

"Give her a kiss," I told Purcell when we said goodbye. "Give her a kiss."

And I can't say I didn't mean it. There are feelings it'd be wrong not to give in to. I'm telling you, it would make the world a better place. We're all victims of prejudice. We lack guts. We lack the guts to say, "Give her a kiss!" But it's saying everything you need to say, the happiness of the world. Purcell agreed. We left as pals. Purcell was my future, my new life. When I got back, I explained everything to L'Espinasse. I went to look for her at the Virginal Secours. She pulled quite a face. So I changed my tune... In that little room I stuck up for myself for the first time in my fucking life, no doubt about it. I didn't have three hours to lose.

"I need the permit," I told her. "You need to give it to me, or else I'll tell the military authorities that you suck off corpses."*

There had been no witnesses. It was pure bluff. She could've reported me to the court martial for slander. Not a single one of those piss-pants on the Saint-Gonzef ward would testify on my behalf. They hadn't seen a thing. They didn't know anything, of course. For starters, they hated me with my stupid medal and the freedom I'd been allowed.

"If you don't give me my R&R, six whole months of sick leave, you understand... I've got nothing to lose... as sure as my name's Ferdinand, I'll come and find you wherever you are and stick my sabre in your guts so deep they'll struggle to get it out. Understood?"

I'd have done it too. I was fighting for my future.

"For England!" I added. "For England!"

"You're not serious, are you, Ferdinand?"

"I am, I am. It's all I think about."

"What will you do there, Ferdinand?"

"Just you mind your own tits," I said, like Cascade.

It was a funny way of talking, but it got me there in the end.

Two days later I left for Boulogne, armed with a beautiful travel permit. I was on my guard at the station. I was on my guard at the port. It was too good to be true. Even my excruciating noises became exciting. I'd never heard anything as magnificent as the ship's horn through my own racket. The ship was waiting for me on the quay. A huffing monster. That morning Purcell and Angèle had already arrived in London. There was no war in London. You couldn't hear the field guns any more. Or barely, just one or two *boom booms* every so often, muffled, way over there, beyond the surf at the water's edge, beyond the sky, you could almost say.

There was lots of civilians on board the ship. They reassured me with their talk of this and that, like before we were condemned to death. They put their meagre belongings in order ahead of the crossing. It was strange and moving to see the ship. Another blast of the horn. That good, that beautiful, that massive ship. A light tremor ran through her entire body, the whole ship vibrated. And immediately the surface of the water in the dock started to vibrate and churn too. We glided along the pitch-black docks and [...] piers. We hit the waves. *Hoop-la!*... We went over the crest. *Hoop-la!*... Keep going!... We went down again. It was raining.

I remember I had seventy francs for this trip. Agathe* had sewn them into my pocket before I left. She was a good girl, after all, was Agathe. We'd meet again.

The two jetties had become tiny, rising just above the foamy white horses, squeezed against the little lighthouse. The town had shrivelled up behind. It dissolved into the sea too. And everything rocked and swayed against the backdrop of the clouds and the enormous shoulders of the open sea. The whole stinking business was over, the entire countryside of France was covered with dung, burying its festering assassins, its groves, its corpses, its multicrapper cities, its endless swarms of myriadshite whizzbangs. All gone. The sea had taken it all, covered it all up. Long live the sea! No more vomiting for me neither. I couldn't. I had enough seasickness inside of me. The war had given me a sea all to myself, a growling, roisterous sea in my own head. Long live the war! The coast had all but vanished. A thin ribbon perhaps, very thin, near the edge of the wind. To the left of the pontoon, way over there, you could still see Flanders. But it was out of sight already.

Matter of fact, I never saw Destinée again. Never even heard what happened to her. The owners of L'Hyperbole must have made a fortune and then sacked her. It's curious. There are people like that. They come from nowhere, toting their load of sentiments as if going to a market. They're trusting and unpack their merchandise any which way. They don't know how to present their stuff. And of course, you don't have the time to go and browse and check their wares. You walk on by, never to turn back. You're in a hurry too. They must feel hurt by that. Maybe they pack up again? Squander what they have? I don't know. What becomes of them? We have no idea. Perhaps they try elsewhere until they have nothing left? And then? Where do they go next? Life is vast, after all. And you get lost everywhere.

Glossary

bint: girl, woman
bog: toilet
bonce: head
butcher's: look
cake hole: mouth
cat house: brothel
conk: nose
dicky bird: word
footslogger: infantry soldier
hawking one's mutton: to work as a prostitute
jizz: sperm
kaput: broken, rendered useless
kisser: mouth, face
Minnie: German trench mortar, from "Minenwerfer"
mutton: deaf
on the game: involved in prostitution
noodle: head
palone: young woman (derogatory)
phiz: face
picon: a kind of bitters commonly drunk with beer
pigs: the police
pine overcoat: coffin
poilu: French infantryman
pong: smell (noun and verb)
pongo: soldier

porky pie: lie
R&R: rest and recuperation
rozzers: the police
schlong: penis
schnozz: nose
schtoom: silent, quiet
Sidi: North African
spunk: sperm
squaddie: soldier
stacked: having big breasts
treacle: sweetheart
turning tricks: to take money for sex
vieux: a Dutch imitation of French cognac distilled from grain or molasses
whizzbang: small-calibre, high-velocity shell
Zouave: light-infantry soldier, originally recruited from Algeria

Note on the Text

This translation is based on the critical edition of *Guerre* published in the Bibliothèque de la Pléiade series of Céline's novels: *Romans, 1932–1947* (Paris: Gallimard, 2023), Vol. 1, pp. 665–752.

Notes

p. 3, *Not quite*. The novel begins *in medias res*. A significant section of possibly nine chapters preceding this one was lost. The missing pages must have contained the story of the narrator and his comrades, who might have been trying to desert and whose ghosts appear later in the novel.

p. 5, *Minnie*: For a list of slang and French words used in this translation, see the Glossary.

p. 8, *"Where are we going?"*: In English in the original.

p. 8, *Yprèss*: Céline's spelling reflects the English pronunciation. It was also called "Wipers" by the British troops.

p. 9, *"I am not going!... the War of Movement!"*: "War of Movement" is a military expression denoting the early phases of the First World War, characterized by clashes taking place in open country, before the front became stabilized and the trench warfare began. The words in italics are in English in the original.

p. 10, *"Brave soldier!... Where do you come from?"*: In English in the original.

p. 10, *where I was coming from*: A mix of English and French in the original: *"d'où que je comais from"*.

p. 15, *Kersuzon, Keramplech, Gargader... Le Cam*: These are all characters from *Cannon Fodder*, Céline's fragmentary novel about his time as an army recruit before the war broke out. They may have played a role in the missing section at the start of *War*. In the first sequence we learn that Kersuzon has died and is lying in a puddle.

p. 16, *King Krogold went back home*: Reference to *The Will of King Krogold* (*La Volonté du roi Krogold*), a legend written by Céline, fragments of which also appear in *Death on Credit*. This is another of the rediscovered works by the author along with a related text called *The Legend of King René* (*La Légende du roi René*). Some of the main characters, in addition to King Krogold, are Gwendor, Wanda, Thibaut and Joad, who are mentioned later on.

p. 18, *stories like that...*: The manuscript contains another page after this that does not appear to belong here, since it tells us that Ferdinand will be operated upon the next day, which does not happen until the second chapter. It cannot be inserted anywhere else in the manuscript and probably comes from another version of the text. The names of the town and hospital are also different. It reads: "'Attention!' I shouted. 'Attention!'.... Louder still. 'Calm down, my friend,' replied the lady, 'calm down... That's it... You are going to drink this and you will not be operated upon until tomorrow morning.' This all happened at the Hospital of the Parfaite-Miséricorde on 22nd January 1915 in Noirceur-sur-la-Lys at around

4 o'clock in the afternoon." Noirceur-sur-la-Lys is also mentioned in *Journey to the End of the Night*.

p. 21, [...]: Here and elsewhere, this notation indicates one or more illegible words in the manuscript.

p. 30, *There was no way of explaining... and how it had ended*: This seems to refer to an episode from before the start of the incomplete manuscript. Mrs Onime may have been the lover of Le Drellière, which would explain why she travels all the way to the front.

p. 32, *he was from the 70th bastion, near Porte Brancion*: At the time Paris was protected by a defensive wall built between 1841 and 1846, the Thiers Wall, which was destroyed after the First World War. Later, the Boulevard Périférique was constructed just outside the former fortifications. The wall consisted of 94 bastions and 17 gates (*portes*). The Porte Brancion was in the XV *arrondissement*, south of Montparnasse.

p. 46, *The poilus we saw... less ceremonial*: In 1915 the French army introduced a new uniform, which was sky blue (*bleu horizon*). The old uniform consisted of red trousers and a blue coat.

p. 46, *It reminded me... which didn't end so well*: In *Death on Credit* the young Ferdinand sells carved goods for a man called Gorloge. In the end he is falsely accused of stealing a golden tiepin.

p. 49, *'Tipperary'*: 'It's a Long Way to Tipperary', a famous English music-hall song, first performed in 1912.

p. 53, *Cascade*: From this point Bébert becomes Cascade, although he is sometimes still referred to by his old name. A Cascade also features in *Guignol's Band*, where he is a pimp in London. A similar figure called Cantaloup appears in *London*, another of the recently rediscovered novels. Bébert is a character in *Journey to the End of the Night*, where he is a young boy whose life Bardamu tries to save in vain. It was also the name of Céline's beloved cat.

p. 59, *They'd pour... between the axles of their vehicles*: There are many corrections in this passage, and the meaning is uncertain.

p. 59, *on the night of 24th November*: The manuscript adds the year 1917, but it is crossed out.

p. 62, *Loulou*: Short for Louis. The main character in *Death on Credit* is called that once too. The author's first name was Louis-Ferdinand.

p. 70, *Marshal Joffre*: Joseph Joffre (1853–1931) was commander-in-chief of the French forces on the Western Front from the start of the First World War until the end of 1916. Céline was awarded a military medal by him in 1914.

p. 77, *her "gammy leg", as she called it*: In *Death on Credit* the narrator's mother, as did Céline's mother in real life, suffers from an atrophied leg.

p. 78, *Célestine*: Later on she will be called Clémence, as in *Death on Credit*.

p. 99, *RAT*: Word play on the acronym for *Réserve de l'armée territoriale*, the reservists of the territorial army.

p. 99, *Les Belles Images*: A children's magazine founded in 1904, also mentioned in *Death on Credit*.

p. 108, *I'm two years older than you, so I'm the one in charge*: Earlier on we learn that Angèle is eighteen.

Ferdinand cannot possibly be sixteen. This is another example of the unredacted state of the manuscript.

p. 116, *"Money!... Money!"*: In English in the original.

p. 116, *"My husband! My husband!"*: In English in the original.

p. 117, *My husband, his*: In English in the original.

p. 118, *engineer*: In English in the original.

p. 121, *KBE*: The text reads "K.B.B.", but Céline probably means KBE, Knight Commander of the Most Excellent Order of the British Empire, even though this order was not created by George V until 1917. This is a different Purcell from the General V. W. Purcell mentioned earlier.

p. 121, *Ingeneers*: This is the spelling in the text.

p. 123, *that you suck off corpses*: These words are crossed out in the manuscript.

p. 124, *Agathe*: Probably a slip for L'Espinasse, whose first name is Aline.